love among the shamrocks collection

Book Two

I0615743

ACROSS THE IRISH SEA

M. KATHERINE CLARK

ISBN-13: 978-0-9998708-1-5

Other Works by
M. Katherine Clark

The Greene and Shields Files:
>   Blood is Thicker Than Water
>   Once Upon a Midnight Dreary
>   Old Sins Cast Long Shadows
>   Tales from the Heart, Novelettes

Soundless Silence a Sherlock Holmes Novel
The Rest is Silence, an Edmond Holmes Novel – Coming Soon
Love Among the Shamrocks Collection:
>   Under the Irish Sky
>   Across the Irish Sea
>   On the River Shannon
>   The Land Across the Sea

Love Among the Shamrocks Collection, The Next Generation:
>   In Dublin Fair City
>   Song of Heart's Desire
>   Chasing After Moonbeams – Coming Soon

The Wolf's Bane Saga:
>   Wolf's Bane
>   Lonely Moon
>   Midnight Sky
>   Star Crossed
>   Moon Rise
>   Moon Song, a Companion

Silent Whispers, a Scottish Ghost Story
Dragon Fire
>   Heart of Fire
>   Will of Fire – Coming Soon

Dedicated to my family and all those who supported me in this wonderful adventure! Thanks to the fans who love Emmet O'Quinn so much, they encouraged me to make Emmet's story unique! Thanks for sticking with me, even though it took a few years!

CHAPTER

ONE

Emmet O'Quinn adjusted his tie and leaned back in his desk chair. Raising his arms, he clasped his hands to the top of his head. The annoying dealership music gnawed on his ears and didn't help his headache. As owner, he intended to do something about it. There's only so many times he could endure *Galway Girl* or *Yellow Brick Road*. The eclectic radio station was new to the area and asked him to be a sponsor to drum up more publicity. As the only dealership and mechanics in ten miles, he agreed. But at that moment, he would rather claw his ears than hear another Irish Jig.

Closing his eyes for a moment to give at least one sensory overload a reprieve, he heard his friend and top salesman come into the office.

"Ya a little soft today, Em?" Paddy asked.

"Nah," Emmet replied. He hadn't finished his one pint last night at the local, so he was far from hung over. "Just a headache, no alcohol involved." No alcohol, but god knew he needed some when he read the letter burning a hole in his cupboard. Even after a week, he still couldn't believe it.

"Hmm, have ye taken anything for it?"

"No," Emmet sighing and opened his eyes, taking his coffee mug. "And since when have you become such a woman? It'll pass soon," he took a gulp of his espresso. Offering a single serve coffee machine out in the waiting area for everyone to use, Emmet kept his espresso maker in his office in case he, Paddy or any other salesman might need a stronger cup than the in bulk Breakfast Blend.

"Want me to take the next ones?" Paddy asked, looking out his window. "A pretty little thing." Emmet raised his head to squint out into the late afternoon sun. "Who's that with her? I can't see from here."

As soon as Emmet's eyes locked on the two women his friend had mentioned, he wished the nineteen eighties linoleum floor would open and drag him down. His ex-fiancée, who was now very much married to his former best friend and five months pregnant with their fourth child, was walking up the drive.

"Oh Jaysus," Emmet breathed. "Of course, why doesn't that surprise me?"

He hadn't seen her for a year. Not since his now sister-in-law, Ness arrived from America and they had gone to Blarney Castle.

"I'd be happy to take this one," Paddy said, eyeing the girl walking beside Chloe.

"I've got it," Emmet replied. Being owner, Emmet could have passed them to someone else, but he didn't like how Paddy was eyeing the woman beside Chloe. "Work is no place to find your next hookup, Paddy." Pulling on his suit jacket, he ran a hand through his auburn hair and went out to greet the two women.

"Chloe," Emmet called, across the parking lot. She looked up and forced a smile.

"Emmet," she greeted when they met halfway. She looked beautiful. Five months pregnant and she glowed. They didn't touch, neither of them offering a hand to each other.

"What brings you out?" He asked.

"My sister, Mara just got back from England and she needs a car to get around. She has a job in Bantry and will be commuting until she's set up." Chloe was saying indicating the younger woman beside her.

The dark-haired woman Paddy had talked about earlier, looked over at him and Emmet's eyes widened.

"Mara?" he asked surprised. "Christ, woman, look at you! You've grown up. You look amazing."

"You don't look too bad yourself, Emmet O'Quinn," she said, her accent subtly Irish.

"How have you been?"

"Good," she answered. "Been in England for a while. Wanted to come back to Ireland when I got the news of Tom's and Chloe's fourth."

"Jaysus," he breathed. "I haven't seen you in, what... at least thirteen years."

"More like fifteen, I think," she said. "I went to Belgium when I was thirteen remember?"

"Saints, I do, girl," he replied. "I remember when you were a child." He couldn't help his eyes trailing over her, taking in all the changes fifteen years had caused. She was beautiful and clearly no longer a child. "You look amazing," he breathed.

Chloe cleared her throat and Emmet felt the weight of her stare. Looking down uncomfortably, he continued. "So, what brings ya to my doorstep?"

"Mara needs a car," Chloe reminded him. "And this is the only dealer near us."

"Right," he replied. "Well, you've come to the right place. What are you looking for?"

"Low emissions, one litre, compact. I'll be staying with Chloe until I can find a place in Bantry," Mara answered.

"You know, a friend of mine down that way is looking to rent the flat over his garage. It's nice. I stayed there for a few months. I think it's only about three hundred euro," he said.

"That sounds pretty perfect actually," she replied.

"I'll give you his number and give him a call, letting him know to expect you," he answered.

"Thanks," she said. "Also, I should say, I need it to be in great nick as I'm not a car mechanic and I don't think I would be comfortable with anything less."

"Ah, I see," Emmet smiled.

"I can't even change a flat," she admitted.

"That's something every girl should know how to do," he said. "I can teach ya."

"I'd like that."

"Tom will be able to teach her, Emmet," Chloe answered.

"Right, of course, sorry," Emmet nodded. "One last question," Emmet turned to Mara again. "Two birds fall out of their nest, one flies, one falls, what kind are they?" She hesitated. "First thing that pops in your mind."

"Robins," she answered. His brows rose. "I know. Stupid."

"Nothing is stupid, just intriguing," he answered. "Follow me."

"Emmet," Chloe called. He turned to her. "I'm sorry. I'm more tired recently. Is there a place I can sit and wait for you?"

"Of course, yeah," he said and waved towards the office. "There's plenty of seats inside. Paddy will help ya."

"Thanks. You good?" she asked her sister. Mara nodded and Chloe headed into the building without another look at Emmet.

He waited for the pang of guilt and perhaps a little jealousy, but it never came. He had loved Chloe, but life put them on separate paths and for once he was glad for her. Tom was a great man. Even if they didn't speak any more, Emmet would always regard him as the best friend he could ever have. Shaking out of his thoughts and turning his attention to the possible sale, he looked back at Mara and they walked together.

"If you don't mind me asking, Emmet," Mara started. "What happened between you and Chloe? You guys were together for nearly five years. Everyone thought you'd get married one day."

"I was an eejit," he answered. "She was too good for me, so I let her go."

"That seems like a very selfless thing to do," Mara said.

"No, it was selfish," he replied. "When we met, I was a kid of sixteen, then my mom died, and I hit a bit of a rough patch in my life. I fell into the wrong crowd and did things I am not proud of. Once that was over, I told Chloe something I regret, and we decided to go our separate ways."

"I'm sorry," Mara said. "It's none of my business. Just one day you were there and the next you were gone, and Chloe was..."

"I know," he breathed. "I would say I'm sorry, but I'm not, because she's with a man who loves her the way she should be loved. Tell me something..." she nodded, and he continued. "Is she happy?"

"Yes," Mara replied. "I won't lie, it was a rough year after you and she broke up and Tom entered the picture. But I know he loves her fiercely and she him. I was angry with you for a long time but then I... don't take this the wrong way... I pitied you. You were always so kind to me and never made me feel like the unwanted baby sister. Chloe had Tom to help her but what about you? You didn't have anyone."

"I didn't need anyone," he lied. "And you were never unwanted. I always enjoyed talking and being around you, even if you were a scrawny little kid," he grinned.

She pretended indignation, slapping him playfully on the arm. "Oh please, at least I grew out of that phase."

"Aye, you did," Emmet stated, his voice low and heavy. "Sorry," he shook his head. "I didn't mean it like that."

"Then how did you mean it?" she questioned, and the timbre of her voice raked up his spine. He scratched the back of his neck and cleared his throat.

"Ehm, enough about me," he said, and she saw a very visible emotional wall go up around him, hiding his true feelings. He stopped in front of the cutest car she'd ever seen. She even like the red color. He crossed his arms over his broad chest and leaned against it. "What do you think?"

"Oh my god!" she exclaimed. "It's adorable!"

"Wanna take it for a drive?" he asked. She nodded emphatically. "I'll go get the keys." Pushing off the car, he headed into the building.

CHAPTER TWO

*D*amn, Emmet thought as he walked into the building to get the keys. Mara was his ex's baby sister and a good eight years younger than him. He repeated those facts again and again, but he couldn't cool his body's response to her. Taking a deep breath, he grabbed the keys out of the wall case. Luckily, he remembered the right ones. Never had he felt such an immediate attraction. True, he had known her for years when they were both kids but that was long ago. She was his ex-fiancée's sister. He was sure somewhere there was a rule written down in stone saying not to angle with that.

Not only could he not afford to be seen with anyone at the moment, he couldn't entertain even for a second, the idea of stepping out with her. Shaking his head to clear it, nothing worked, and he was highly tempted to ask Paddy to help her with the test drive. But even that thought caused a jealous streak he never had before, to race through him so fast he shivered. Any other time he would be interested to explore the feelings stirring inside him, but he was neither free to do so nor would he allow himself to hurt another McGrath woman.

7

Still consumed by his thoughts as he walked back out to the parking lot, he was surprised to see Mara looking angrily at her phone. She punched a message and hit send. Putting it into her purse, she looked up at him and immediately, seeing a sort of angry fear behind her brown eyes, he rushed to her.

"Everything all right?"

"Great," she answered quickly.

Normally not one to pry but after the adventures with Ness, his sister-in-law, almost a year ago, he didn't like it when a woman had that look. It usually meant they were hiding something or from someone and in over their head.

"Mara," he challenged.

She must have sensed the change because her shoulders deflated, and she finally spoke. "My ex, he won't give up."

"He sounds like an arse," Emmet replied.

"You don't know the half of it," she nonchalantly touched her cheek and Emmet froze. He tried to push away the thought of her touching a place the bastard had bruised often. Still not in a position to do more than distract her, he held out the keys.

"Well," he said tightly. "How about a test drive, then?"

"Sounds good," she smiled.

He tossed her the keys but she shielded her face and the keys fell to the ground.

"I'm sorry. Are you all right?"

"I'm fine, sorry." Reaching down, she picked up the key and without another word, slid in the driver's side.

Explaining some of the features of the car, Emmet watched her through the corner of his eye. Even though she seemed interested in everything he was explaining, he could tell she was still shaken by the text she had received and possibly, him throwing the keys to her. He decided to put the salesman on hold and leaned back in his seat.

"Pull off up here," he said gently.

She looked over at him but agreed. He guided her to the entrance of a parking lot and into one of the spots. Emmet got out and walked around to her side. Opening her door, he offered his hand to help her out. They walked a little way until they came to the top of a small rise.

"Oh my," she sighed. "Emmet, this is beautiful."

"One of my favorite views," he said thinking of how many views he deemed were his favorite. He had shared at least three with Ness over a year ago.

"It's so... secluded," she said, then suddenly looked wary. "Why did you bring me here, alone?"

"I thought you might like it," he shrugged, hating the images flicking through his mind as to why she was so scared.

"Is anyone around?" she wrapped her arms around herself and took a few steps away from him.

"There's a lot of people around," he answered.

She visibly relaxed when he pointed out a couple old fishermen and a father and son bringing in their early afternoon catch.

Seeing the natural beauty of County Kerry, he watched as she relaxed. That is, until her phone vibrated in her handbag. She tried to ignore them but after the twelfth one, Emmet look over at her.

"Sounds important," he said.

"He's not," she stated. "He's just a bastard who needs to learn his favorite toy fights back and if he ever lays another hand on me."

"Did he hit you?" Emmet questioned.

She pursed her lips together and didn't turn to him, but

he saw the tears in her eyes. When her phone buzzed for the nineteenth time, she let out a strange cry and dug for it. She nearly chucked it into the water, when Emmet grabbed her wrist to stop her.

She shrieked and struck his chest. "Let me go!"

"Easy, Mara," he immediately dropped his hand from her wrist. "I'm not gonna hurt you."

Almost immediately, Mara's whole body shook and fell into him. Her scream was muffled by his shirt and she struck his chest, not hurting him. Shaking her head back and forth, she cried out and he felt the wet tears on his shirt. Hating it when women cried, Emmet wrapped his arms around her and held her close. No man should ever raise his hand to a woman, nor make her cry in fear. His jaw ticked as he gritted his teeth hard. If he knew who the bastard was, he would gather his brothers together, all of whom were raised the same way, and they would track him down. The man would wish he'd never met Mara when they were finished with him. His father always taught him how to treat a woman, with respect and love. Make her cry from joy not fear or pain, he would say. She should be cherished.

"I'm sorry," she said, her words interrupted by hiccups.

"It's all right," he answered. "I'm here. My sister-in-law went through something similar a year ago. But she is strong, just like you and she was able to get through it. Of course, she had me to help," he winked.

She laughed breathlessly. "You can't fight my battles for me, Emmet."

"No, but I can be here for you."

She gazed up into his eyes. He knew he should pull back, but when she licked her lips, he couldn't stop himself. Leaning down to capture her lips in a kiss, he waited to see if she would stop them. When she didn't, he closed his eyes, feeling just the briefest of touches when her phone buzzed three times in her hand making them both jump and breaking the spell between them.

What in the bloody hell am I doing? Emmet demanded. He pulled away so quickly, he worried she would fall. "I'm sorry, I shouldn't have done that. We should get back," Emmet said. *And quickly,* he thought.

"You're right, I'm sorry. I was feeling vulnerable and needed someone," Mara said putting her phone back in her handbag. "Thank you, Emmet, for not taking advantage."

"I would have, had your phone not dinged."

"I would have let you," she admitted. Heading to the driver's side of the car, she didn't look at him when she opened the door and got in.

Emmet sighed harshly, *not good,* he thought. The faster they got back to the dealer the better. He had to get Mara McGrath out of his head.

Benjamin watched from his car up the road as Mara and the redheaded giant got back into the cheap little red car. He nearly pulled out his gun from the glove compartment when he saw the man try to kiss her. She was his and no other man could ever have her. Ever since he saw her singing at that little pub in London, he knew he had to have her. When he got her the job, it was like he struck gold even if she didn't know his full involvement in her hiring. But after what she did to him, he looked forward to exacting his revenge.

Ducking down as they passed, he slowly pulled out and followed at a safe distance. Mara should never have crossed him, she didn't know who she was dealing with. She had it good. He always spoiled his women, gave them everything they wanted. He only asked for a little loyalty in return. *Loyalty...* he scoffed. She didn't know what it meant. He would be happy to make her feel the same desperation he felt. *Soon,* he thought. *Soon, it would be over.*

CHAPTER
THREE

Chloe found her way inside the office building. Recognizing Paddy from a long time ago, she called to him. He turned with a brilliant smile that faltered when he saw her.

"Chloe?" by the time he said her name, his smile had all but disappeared. "It's been a while."

"It has," she answered. "I didn't realize you worked here. I thought you were still at the Plaza."

"I am," he replied. "But it's the off season. Cutting hours."

"Oh, of course," she said. "You look good."

"Thanks," he replied tightly. "What can I do for you?"

"Is there a reason you are so abrupt with me?" she questioned. Sometimes she cursed pregnancy hormones, but not at that moment.

"What would you have me say?" he asked. "I saw what my friend went through when you married his best friend."

"What *he* went through?" she demanded. "You may want to reconsider your choice of words, Paddy O'Shea."

"I chose my words carefully."

"Then you are misinformed. I would be married to him right now if he hadn't ended it. So, I am unsure as to why you are treating me with such distain."

Paddy's brows furrowed for a moment but soon the cool mask of indifference settled on his features. "If you are looking for an apology, you won't receive one."

"I wasn't looking for either an apology nor condemnation, especially not from you Paddy," she said. "Now, I happen to be very tired and Emmet said there was a seat I could have to wait for them. If you can simply point me in the correct direction, I would be happy to get out of your hair."

"His office is right over there. I'm sure he wouldn't mind if you waited there."

"Thank you," she answered. "And for the record," she turned back to him. "Emmet cheated on me then broke up with me. Tom has always been there. I love him more than anything. I would appreciate it if you never said that to me again."

Paddy said nothing and she headed into Emmet's office. Tears threatened. She hated the ups and downs of her emotions. But Paddy used to be a complete gentleman. Rogue but gentleman, nonetheless. Shaking her head, it wasn't worth anymore time. She and Tom had been married for eleven years and she was happier than she ever dreamt. It wasn't worth the effort to correct Paddy's misconception, instead, she closed the door to Emmet's office and nearly gagged. His cologne hung heavy in the air and as much as she used to love it, now, with every other sense heightened, she needed some fresh air. Opening the door again, she breathed deeply, smiling when she caught herself thinking how Tom's cologne never smelled stale to her. Maybe she was over Emmet O'Quinn after all.

She looked over and saw water bottles on the side board beneath an expanse of cupboards. Grabbing a bottle, she jumped when something fell out of one of the doors overhead. Seeing it was something important with the return address of the DNA Diagnostic Center, she did not pry and opened the cupboard to put it back inside.

She froze when she saw an old photograph taped to the inside of the cupboard. Recognizing herself and Emmet both younger, standing at St. Stephen's Green smiling, a fond memory came over her, it was the day he proposed to her. Tom had taken the photo but as much as she tried to remember the details of that day, all she remembered was the day when Tom proposed to her. He was her future and Emmet, her past. But if the way he was looking at Mara was any indication, she may have to warn her sister about the effects he has on women and more importantly his player approach to everyone.

"Chloe," Emmet's voice caused her to jump. She turned and saw a questioning gaze reflected in his eyes. Realizing she was staring at the photograph taped inside the cupboard and still held the envelope in her hand, a flush of color rose to her cheeks.

"I'm so sorry," she muttered. "This fell out and it looked important, so I opened the door to put it back. I didn't mean to pry."

He nodded and his eyes turned down to the envelope in her hands. He swallowed unconsciously. Thanking her, he extended his hand to take the envelope from her. Shutting the cupboard door and heading to his wall safe, nothing gave his emotions away, but she knew him too well not to see the tension in his broad shoulders or the tilt of his head, signs he was apprehensive. Quickly putting the envelope away, he walked around to his side of the desk and Chloe turned to her sister, standing in the doorway. Mara's eyes were red, and Emmet had a clear mascara stain on his light blue oxford shirt as if he held her while she cried.

Knowing firsthand how Emmet's embrace could remove any demons around her, she gently touched her sister's arm. "Is everything okay?" Chloe asked her.

Mara nodded but said nothing. Her eyes gave it away. She had gotten another text. Keeping her sister's secret had been one of the hardest things when Tom had asked what was going on, but he understood the bond of blood and dropped it when she told him she was sworn to secrecy. Still, the texts were getting worse and Chloe worried it was only a matter of time before her sister's past caught up to them.

"So, Mara," Emmet said turning to them and bringing Chloe's focus back to the present. "Please sit. Do you like the car?" She nodded again and smiled slightly. "Then let's see if we can get it for you."

"Why the hell did you let her in my office?" Emmet demanded from Paddy after Mara left in her new car with Chloe following behind.

Paddy looked up, unfazed by his outburst. Luckily, everyone else that worked there had gone home for the day and it was just the two of them.

"Where else was I supposed to put her?" Paddy asked sarcastically.

"Keep her out here, put her in the waiting room but keep her the hell out of my office!"

"Afraid your little shrine was discovered?"

"You're an arse," Emmet replied.

"Of course I am," he sighed. "I'm the only one here you don't intimidate. And what is this about *you* breaking up with her?"

"Go to hell, Paddy," Emmet stalked out of the room and went outside. The fresh air stirred his bones and cleared his mind.

His initial thoughts ran to the envelope Chloe had found. Thank god she hadn't looked inside. No one could know what was in that envelope, yet. Hell, he didn't want to know.

Closing his eyes, he took another cleansing breath and pushed those thoughts aside. Turning to something far more complicated, Mara. Even though their meeting had been interesting to say the least, she had stirred something within him that lain dormant for over a year. She needed help and he wanted to be the one to support her. He wanted to know what happened to her. Before she left, he made sure to give her his card, stressing if she ever needed him, to give him a call. He would answer day or night. Her forced smile, then subtle side-glance to Chloe waiting a respectable distance, made him nod and take a step back. He would never want to pit sister against sister, but she needed to know he was there for her, as he would be for any woman in need. He may be known as a player but when it came to the safety of his ladies, he would drop everything to take care of them.

Checking his watch, he shrugged. *Close enough.* He had purchased his dealership from Old Larkin when he retired and added a maintenance garage, as the nearest one was in Bantry Bay. A couple years he had been in the red, but with good help and a good economy, he was turning profits left and right. So much so, he was going to need to hire another sales rep.

Heading back inside to tell Paddy to close up, he grabbed his coat and car keys. He needed a pint. Almost as if she knew, his phone rang *Born in the USA* as soon as he got into his car.

"Hiya beautiful, where have you been all my life?" He asked.

His sister-in-law Ness giggled on the other end. "Sorry, handsome, I'm taken," she replied.

"Pity," he lamented. Her laugh was music to him and lightened his mood tremendously. Over a year had passed since she had arrived on Ireland's Shore but the circumstances surrounding her time there under the Irish sky were well ingrained in his memory. Since then, she had married his youngest brother Sean and they were expecting their first child by the end of next month. "How you doing, *cailín*?" He knew she loved it when he called her *girl* in his native language.

"Oh, you know, just waiting for next month," she sighed.

"How is my nephew treating you?"

"He's been a bit active," she admitted. "But Sean has been marvelous. He's cleaning the house right now, making me put my feet up. I'm so glad we are having this little lad in the summer when Sean can be home with me."

"Good on him," Emmet smiled, grateful for the tenth time Sean had seen sense last year and married Ness instead of Trisha allowing him not only the happiness he so deserved, but the ability to keep his job at the county school, instead of moving to Dublin.

"But I wanted to call my *other* favorite Irishman and see how you were doing."

"I guess I can settle for second best," he chuckled.

"Second only to my husband and father of this little rascal. But I've put in some Shepherd's Pie, only to realize I made far too much for just the two of us. I thought you might want to come over," she offered.

"Oh aye, woman, you know the way to me heart."

"I try," she giggled again. "Have to keep my Irishmen happy."

"In more ways than one."

"Och, you rogue."

"I don't want to know why Sean always has a smile on his face every single time I see him. It's nasty," he teased.

She laughed even harder. "Stop! You're going to make me pee."

"More work for Sean," he replied.

"He loves me, but I don't think he'd be very happy cleaning up."

"Perhaps," he answered. "What time do you want me over?"

"When are you leaving work?"

"I'm actually in my car now."

"Oh, that's early."

"The day was strange."

"In a good way?"

"Ehm, no," he answered. "Which is why I could use a dose of my favorite girl."

"Well, it won't be done for another thirty minutes but that'll be enough time for you to get here and start a beer," she said.

"Sounds like the best night," he replied, starting his car. "I'll be there in fifteen."

CHAPTER FOUR

Mara deleted the texts on her phone without reading them, uninterested in what Ben had to say to her. Taking a deep breath, she tried to focus her mind on something else. Her little car was wonderful and Emmet got her a great deal.

Emmet...

Just the thought of his name sent a shiver down her back. She didn't realize she was smiling until her cheeks started to hurt.

Then, the realization of who he was; the man who broke her sister's heart, poured over her and she didn't like the feelings stirring inside her. As a cocky youth, when she found out what Emmet had done to Chloe, she swore vengeance but when she grew older, she realized lovers come and go. Chloe had the best revenge... she moved on.

But seeing him today, she saw just what it was Chloe loved about him. And like Icarus, she felt she had flown too close to the sun and was falling hard.

"Mara," Chloe called to her. "Tom'll be here with dinner soon."

"Be right there!"

Plugging her phone into the charger, she headed to the door. Just as she was about to leave, her phone rang a generic ring tone. Sighing, she went over to her phone again, not recognizing the number. As she had just bought a car, she answered.

"Hello?" No one spoke immediately. "Hello?" Then like out of some sick horror movie, she heard heavy breathing. "Who is this?" she demanded. "You're disgusting whoever you are. Never call me again."

"Hello, Mara," a voice said. The voice she never wanted to hear again. Ben's voice. The man from her nightmares. The man who preyed on her. Before she could think, she reacted. Flinging the phone away from her, she raced down the stairs, tripping on the last stair. Screeching, she fell on her bum just as Tom walked in through the front door.

"Mara?" he questioned. "Are you okay? Is everything all right? Chlo!"

Chloe was rushing as fast as she could from the living area. "Mara, honey?" Chloe asked. "What happened?"

Mara couldn't catch her breath. Her chest burned with fear, dread and pain. Her bum hurt too, but that was from falling on it.

"Ben," she barely got out.

Chloe and Tom looked at each other. All Chloe had told him was Mara was running from a man named Ben.

"Where?" Tom demanded. When she didn't answer, he bent down and grasped her shoulders gently but firmly. "Where, Mara?"

"Phone," she answered.

Tom released her and looked back at his wife. "Are the

children inside?"

"They're with your parents."

He reached back into his pocket and grabbed his keys. "Good." Heading towards the closet door, he unlocked the gun rack and grabbed his hunting rifle, making sure it was loaded. Careful to lock the rack up again, he turned to the two women.

"Tommy, don't be a fool," Chloe called to him.

"We'll never truly be safe until we know he's not here," he said. "Stay inside and lock this door after me."

"Tom," Chloe cried.

He turned suddenly and kissed her hard. She moaned into his mouth as tears ran down her cheeks. Tearing his mouth away, his forehead rested on hers.

"Do this for me, love," he pleaded. She nodded, her eyes still closed. "I love you," he said, then was gone.

Tom left with the large gun slung over his arm. Chloe gasped and clutched at her belly.

"Chlo?" Mara panicked, jumping up and rushing to her sister.

"I'm fine," she answered. Mara helped her to sit down in the living room and knelt in front of her.

"I'm so sorry," Mara said.

"Mar, stop, it's all right," Chloe said. "You're my little sister, stop worrying."

"But if I hadn't have come back, none of this would have—"

"Where would you have gone?" Chloe asked taking her hand. "We're sisters. You will always have me."

She clutched at her sister's hand and smiled faintly. Both women jumped when her phone rang again. Angrily, Mara grasped it and answered.

"Listen to me, you little plonker. I don't know who you think you are, but if you ever call me again, I'll cut your bollocks off and feed them to my dogs. The things you have put my sister through is inexcusable. How dare you do this to us! You will never have me. If you ever see me on the street, keep walking because I never want to see your ugly face again! Do I make myself clear?" Mara didn't stop. "Oh and another thing, you were never *that* good in bed, it was all faked. Do you understand me?"

There was silence on the other end of the phone. Then, "yeah, I get it," a voice said harshly.

Mara went pale as the line disconnected. "Emmet?" She gasped.

CHAPTER
FIVE

A few minutes earlier

"Emmet," Ness smiled and opened her arms to him. "It is so wonderful to see you!"

Stepping over the threshold, he embraced her as tightly as he could with her eight-month pregnant, protruding belly in the way. Ness made a happy sigh when she pulled back.

"I've missed you," she said.

"You just saw me Sunday," he teased.

"Three whole days!" She cried. "That's like eternity to a pregnant woman!"

"Well, I want the newlyweds to get their sappy romantic shite over with without a witness," he teased.

"Oh, listen to you, newlyweds... it's been a year!"

"That's still newlyweds," Emmet winked.

"Tiss," she replied with a sound learned directly from

Emmet's and Sean's stepmother. "You look well."

"And you look magnificent," he answered. "Sean, you lucky bastard." His eyes turned up to his brother walking up behind his wife.

"I know it well," Sean smirked, wrapping his arm around his wife's waist and dropping a kiss on her red hair.

"Awe, I love you, baby," Ness leaned into him and gave him a sweet look. "Come in, come in," Ness turned back to Emmet and stepped aside, still tucked under Sean's arm. "Dinner is almost ready." She pulled away from her husband with a kiss on his cheek and went to the kitchen.

Emmet cleared the entryway and embraced his brother. "Good to see ya," Sean slapped his brother's back in an affectionate gesture. "Pint?"

"Parched," Emmet replied.

"Come on then. Ness has kicked me out of the kitchen. Apparently, I hover too much," Sean smiled.

Emmet laughed but followed his brother down the hall and into the kitchen. Sean looked good. He was happy, content in a way Emmet had never seen him before. Opening the door to the refrigerator, Sean pulled out two bottles of beer.

"Out, out both of you," Ness teased and tapped her husband's bum as he leaned over the refrigerator door.

"Ooh, love," Sean grinned eyeing her. "Not when we have company," he winked.

"That's just nasty," Emmet said as he saw Ness grin and bite her lower lip.

"We'll be out back, darlin'," Sean called over his shoulder.

"Not without a kiss, you're not," Ness stated.

Sean looked over at Emmet, his eyes dancing in amusement. "Oh, the things I must do."

Giving the two of them privacy, Emmet headed out the back door to the deck. Their father, Orin, was a master craftsman and carpenter. When Ness and Sean decided on a house but didn't care for the slab of concrete that served as the back deck, Orin had built his son and new daughter-in-law a lovely deck, knowing how much they enjoyed having family and friends over. Emmet had to admit, he was a tiny bit envious of the beautiful workmanship. Walking to the edge of the deck, he rested his hands on the railing and gazed out to the copse of trees, lining their yard.

Mara was in his head. He couldn't seem to get her out. He had been itching to call her since she left. Maybe he could when he got back home... if it wasn't too late.

"What's her name?" Sean's voice behind him, startled him.

Looking back, Emmet saw his baby brother leaning against the door frame. Ness hummed along to a song as she worked behind him in the kitchen. Eight years age difference and another brother between them, Sean and Emmet had never been every close. But after the events over a year ago involving Ness, Sean's then fiancée Trisha and their brother Innis, they grew much closer.

"What? Who?" Emmet asked.

Sean pushed off the doorway and walked over. "The girl you were pining over just now."

"I don't pine," Emmet replied.

"Whatever you say," Sean popped the tab on both beers in his hand and offered his brother one of them.

"Sláinte," they both said, knocking the necks together before taking a long swig.

"So..." Sean pressed. "Who is she?"

Emmet sighed. There was no getting out of it. Since his brother had married, he had become worse than an old biddy at a knitting session, always wanting his one unmarried brother to

25

find the happiness he enjoyed.

"The person I *think* you're asking me about is Mara," Emmet admitted.

"How'd you meet?" Sean asked.

"Marriage has really turned you into an old woman, Sean," Emmet grumbled. Sean chuckled and took another drink. "If you must know, she bought a vehicle off me today."

"Grand," Sean replied. "Is she pretty?"

"Very," Emmet sighed.

"And?"

"And what?"

"Did you get her number? Are you going to see her again?"

"It's complicated."

"How so?" Sean asked.

"Well, for starters, she's Chloe's baby sister." Emmet let that sink in as he took another swig from his beer. Sean nearly choked on his drink.

He was a child, same age as Mara when Emmet first met Chloe but when they broke up, Sean was at school and didn't know all that transpired. Over the years, Sean learned the gist of it and clearly remembered who Chloe was.

"Ehm..." he cleared his throat. "Emmet, you really know how to pick 'em."

"Don't you think I know? I would have gotten her in bed and moved on to the next one by now," Emmet sighed.

"You think it's only lust, then?"

"No, not *only*. That's the other thing," Emmet said. "I haven't felt like this in a long time, like."

"That's good," Sean replied taking a drink.

"Chloe's *sister*, Sean?"

"Hey, what can I say? You have odd taste in women, so you do."

"Cheers," Emmet answered taking a drink of his beer.

"Why don't you call her? I mean, Ness said it'll be about ten minutes until the food's ready. Call her. Setup a time to go to the pub. Go on. What's the worst that can happen? She says no? Then you're no better or worse off than you are now, like," Sean reasoned.

"I can't, you know that."

"You can still call her," Sean pressed. "No one can fault you for wanting to call a pretty girl."

Emmet thought a moment, he did not want to let an opportunity with Mara pass him by, but he was not in a position to make any promises. The letter in the envelope Chloe found, rang in his ears. He was so close to the end. Still, he didn't want to let her go. Pulling out his phone, Emmet found her number on the dealer database, chuckling to himself, thinking how stalkerish he was becoming. He also had to remind himself what he said to Paddy earlier, about work not being a place to find the next hookup.

Feeling his brother's eyes on him, Emmet said nothing, but when Mara answered, she didn't give him a moment to say who he was before she started yelling at him. Emmet's blue eyes grew stormy and his jaw clenched tightly. When his knuckles grew white around his beer, Sean took a step toward him, concerned.

"Yeah, I get it," Emmet finally said, then hung up.

Letting loose a string of expletives, Emmet chucked his phone into the grass. How could she say those things to him? Did she not realize he was just as affected by the whole situation as she was? As Chloe was? He never wanted to have feelings for his ex's sister, but it happened. Christ, the things she said! She shredded any form of dignity he had. How could anyone be so cold? Was it the almost kiss? Was it the picture in the cupboard? What had caused the change? Had Chloe really faked everything? Jaysus, that was the real blow to his dignity. *Do women even talk about that?* He wondered.

His phone rang from somewhere in the grass. He never wanted to use it again. It was a mistake. How could he have ever thought something could happen between them? There was far too much history.

His phone rang again. *Let it,* he thought. *It doesn't matter.* He didn't want to answer in case it was her again. He didn't think his manhood could handle another direct blow.

Turning to his brother, he saw Sean's concerned gaze but said nothing. Emmet gulped down his beer to alleviate some of the tension in his gut but oddly it was pain in his chest that drew his attention. He hated that feeling and refused to think it could be what it was. Heartbreak.

"Dinner's ready, boys," Ness's voice rang through the door.

Emmet had no stomach for food, but he would not do that to Ness. Forcing a smile, he turned to the door. Before they went in, he stopped and looked at Sean.

"Not a word to Ness," he said. Sean nodded once and followed his brother into the kitchen.

CHAPTER
SIX

"Emmet?" Chloe questioned, shocked when she heard her sister name him.

"Oh my god!" Mara was sick. "What he must be thinking right now!" All her words came back to her and she clutched her stomach as dry heaves chased up her throat.

"What happened today?" Chloe asked. "Emmet is a good salesman but to call you so quickly seems a bit excessive."

"There was an incident today while driving around, and, oh god, please answer," she called back and put her hand to her forehead.

"Are you all right? What sort of incident?"

Mara cursed when the phone rang out and went to voicemail. "Ben texted me about fifteen times in thirty seconds and it made me angry and scared," she answered. "Emmet... helped me."

"Did you tell him?" Chloe asked.

"Not all of it. He just... held me as I cried."

"Oh sweetie, you never cry," Chloe reached for her sister's hand. Mara sat down beside her on the couch and fiddled with her phone, typing out a text.

"I know," Mara answered. "But I felt safe with him."

"You have history, we all do. I'm sure I would feel the same. I just don't want to see you hurt."

"I know sis, and I'm sorry for everything. This isn't any better, I know. What with your history with Emmet, I'm sure you didn't ever want to hear his name again."

"I loved Emmet, you know that," Chloe answered. "But Ireland is a very small island and our village is even smaller. If I absolutely had to get away from Emmet O'Quinn, then I should have moved. I'm fine, Mar, just be careful."

Mara nodded giving her sister a soft smile as she dialed again and waited. Still nothing. This time though, she left a message. "Emmet, it's Mara, listen that wasn't meant for you. As you know, we're having some problems with my ex and he called me tonight. Kinda freaked me out and scared Chloe. I swear, I thought it was him calling me back. I didn't mean to say those things to you. Please, when you get this, call me back? Please. I really want to explain what happened. Please believe me." Hanging up, she lowered her head to her hands. "Oh god, the things I said to him."

"He's a big boy," Chloe said. "He can handle it."

"I'll try again."

"Mara, don't. Emmet doesn't like to be pestered," Chloe said. "He'll come around and listen to the voicemail. Then, if he wants to, he'll call you again."

"You're right, but it doesn't help."

"Believe me, I know there's nothing like not being able to get a hold of him when you want to talk."

Mara looked down, she remembered her sister crying

and trying to call Emmet every half-hour one time when he told her they needed a break.

"Chloe?" Tom called from the front door.

"We're in here, Tommy," she answered. Then looking at her sister, she lowered her voice, "please don't tell him about Emmet." Mara agreed.

After a moment, putting the gun away, Tom came into the room and went straight to his wife.

"I'm all right," she reassured when he knelt in front of her and framed her face, kissing her gently.

"Would someone tell me what the hell is going on?" he demanded taking her hands in his.

"Long story," Mara answered typing out a text on her phone.

"I've got all night," he growled looking sharply over at Mara. "Put down that damn phone for once in your life and tell me what the hell is going on!"

"Tommy, calm down," Chloe squeezed his hands.

"No, no' a chance," he stated. "This is getting ridiculous. Don't give me any excuses. I want to know what really is going on. All of it."

Mara looked over at Chloe and took a deep breath. Setting her phone down on the coffee table, she stood, paced and finally turned to her brother-in-law.

"You remember when I was in an accident in London?" She started. At his nod, she continued. "Well, that's not exactly true."

"Excellent, as always, Nessie," Emmet teased Ness as he leaned back in his chair at the kitchen table. Taking his teacup with him, he patted his flat stomach.

"You know I hate that name." Ness grinned and slapped his arm lovingly.

"Yeah," he answered. "But no' when I say it." He winked at her and Sean chuckled. "Better watch out, Sean. You might get dad's belly with all of Ness's good cooking." Sean laughed and raised his teacup in cheers. Their father hardly had a large stomach but he always teased their stepmother about how good her cooking was.

"Ha," Ness answered. "You know, I would be happy to have Sean wind up like your father. He's such a sweetie."

"A sweetie?" Emmet raised an eyebrow and looked at Sean. "Well, that's one way of putting it."

"Da' loves her, you know that," Sean drank his tea.

"And who doesn't?" Emmet smiled at her.

"Oh stop," Ness giggled. "But..." she teased. "One thing I've learned after a year of being married to an O'Quinn, is to never question you."

"That's right, lass," Emmet grinned. "We're always right."

"Oh? I doubt your ma would agree," Ness replied.

"She loves me," Emmet shrugged. "She'll always side with me."

"Oh, is that a fact?" she laughed taking the dessert platter and passing it to Sean. "I suppose we women are suckers for those dancing eyes of yours, Em."

"My women love me," he replied simply helping himself to two lemon squares from the plate Sean passed to him.

"Speaking of your women," Ness began. "Are you going to tell me what's going on?"

Emmet's side-glance at Sean told her everything she needed to know.

"Not sure I know what you mean, love," Emmet replied.

"Oh, now I *know* something is going on," she stated. "You only call me *love* when you are hiding something."

"Not true," he answered. "I call you *love* all the time."

"Mmhmm," she replied. "Truthfully though, Emmet," she sobered. "I know something happened outside between you two. My husband's eyes give far too much away." Sean leaned back and looked at her innocently. "Don't deny it, I could read you the moment I met you." Ness covered Sean's hand and smiled lovingly at him. Turning her attention back to Emmet, she continued. "I love you both so much and you helped me through my darkest times, I want to help you with yours. We're family Emmet. Did something happen with Trevor?"

Emmet's eyes shot up to hers. He had yet to share the final contents of the envelope with his family and looking at Ness, he realized that was a mistake, lying was so much more difficult.

"No nothing," he lied.

"Then tell me," Ness pried.

Emmet closed his eyes and launched into the story from the beginning. He was grateful Ness listened to the whole thing without interrupting, although he felt her tense when he told her about the phone call. When he finally finished, he grabbed his teacup and drank some of the lukewarm liquid.

Ness took a deep breath before speaking and looked above him at the far wall as if gathering her thoughts. Finally, she took the tea pot and poured Sean and herself some more.

"Well," she said as she set the pot down. "You are handling it well."

"Yeah well," Emmet shrugged. "It's not every day I get my bollocks handed to me."

Ness slowly raised her teacup to her lips and took a drink before she answered.

"You know," she started. "Not to play devil's advocate, or

whatever it is you guys say over here… but what if, just humor a pregnant lady, hmm?" she set her tea down. "What if she didn't know it was you calling? You said she was having problems with that ex of hers. What if something happened between the time you two were together and now?"

"Ness, love, I gave her my number," Emmet said.

"No," Ness shook her head. "You gave her your *card*. She may not have programmed it in yet, and maybe she didn't look at the name. Listen," Ness sighed. "When I was going through the hardest part of my life just over a year ago, you said some things to me I didn't particularly agree with or like, but I listened to you because you are my best friend. And you know what? You ended up being absolutely right. Now, I am asking you to listen to me," she reached over and rested her hand over his. "Go get your phone and see if she's called. Answer the phone next time and let her explain. Trust me, there is nothing worse than not being able to explain things to the man you love."

"She doesn't love me, Ness," Emmet said.

"Maybe not yet," she smiled. "But trust me, I know what she's going through right now. Get your phone."

Emmet sighed harshly and looked over at his brother. Sean's stupid grin was wide as he raised his hands and shrugged.

"I've learned not to argue with my wife," Sean said. "But, I also agree with her. You need to be sure. Don't spend another ten years wondering *what if.*"

Emmet looked from one to the other and sighed harshly, pushing away from the table.

"Fine," he stood. "I give up." Sean followed him out with a flashlight. Emmet's phone beeped somewhere in the darkness indicating he had a message. They followed the sound and eventually found his phone. Luckily, the ground was not wet, and his phone was relatively unharmed. But the missed calls were in the double digits and there was a couple dozen text messages. Sean looked over his brother's shoulder and chuckled.

"Looks like someone is trying to get a hold of you."

"Maybe," Emmet replied. "Look I really don't want to check the voicemails, but I know Ness won't let me get away from them. Cover for me?"

"You want me to sleep on the sofa?" Sean raised an eyebrow. "Sorry, Em, I love sleeping with my wife a wee bit too much to lie for you, so I do."

"I cannot blame you for that," Emmet replied then sighed. "Well, I am going to head home. Better go and say goodbye to my favorite American."

"Good luck getting out without checking that phone, like," Sean teased slapping his brother on the back as they walked into the house.

CHAPTER
SEVEN

Mara couldn't sleep. Tossing and turning and switching on the television didn't help. Finally, she lay in darkness completely awake. Groaning, she turned over, and buried her face in her pillow as she remembered the look in Emmet's eyes as he gazed down at her on the river bank. He caused her heart, mind and body to react in a way she never wanted with him.

Turning back over, she covered her eyes with her arm. She was no blushing virgin with her first crush, so why was she acting like one? Sitting up, she brushed her hair back. What was it about him that made the McGrath women weak at the knees?

Checking the time, her phone's lock screen was empty of calls or texts. As the minutes ticked over to three in the morning, she decided to get a glass of warm milk. Sliding to the edge of the bed, she was about to stand when her phone buzzed on the nightstand. Jumping at the sound, she raced across the bed and checked the name she had programmed after the fifth time calling.

Fumbling, she answered breathlessly, "Emmet?"

"Hiya," he replied softly.

"Thank god," she sighed. "I am so sorry, really Emmet. I never meant... it wasn't directed at you at all."

"I know," Emmet replied. "I got your texts and voicemails."

"I'm so sorry," she said. "What you must be thinking right now. Believe me, nothing I said could even be remotely about you. Chloe never said a single bad thing about you. Really Emmet, I never... it wasn't meant for you."

Sighing harshly, he went on. "Do you want to tell me what's going on?"

She flopped back down onto her bed. "Yes," she answered. "I think I owe you that."

He didn't say anything, waiting. Plunging ahead, she closed her eyes as if it would change what she was saying.

"When I left school a few years ago, I wanted to be a singer but all the gigs I had were not paid and I was having a hard time making ends meet. I was too proud to come back home and ask my family for help since they were not exactly happy I dropped out of University. I eventually realized I needed a job but also the freedom to play my gigs when I had them. I applied for a part time secretary for a rather lucrative stock broker firm in London. It was good pay but still not enough. Not for London and I was barely making ends meet.

"One of the junior partners took a fancy to me and started sending me flowers, chatting and eventually asked me out. He was cute and I hardly knew anyone, so I agreed. We started seeing each other and we... I'll spare you no details, but we began sleeping together. I didn't know he was married when we started. He never wore a ring and he never talked about his wife or kids. There weren't pictures in his office either. His wife found me and told me the truth. I was just another in a long line of others and she asked me, rather nicely I thought, to please

37

leave him. She was going to file for divorce as soon as she could and asked me to be a witness for her. I agreed. I was so angry with him. When he came over that night, I confronted him about. It was the first time he hit me. I'll never forget his face when I was called to testify at the divorce case, pictures of my bruised face on display for everyone to see.

"When the judge ruled in favor of his wife in the amount of three hundred thousand pounds and a month in prison for his attack on me, Ben lost it. He yelled he would kill me. I was visited by several police officers later that month telling me when he got out of prison, he had vanished. They were keeping tabs on him. He had missed his payment to his wife and of course what he did to me. Later that night, he found his way into my flat and terrorized me. He beat me so badly I only woke up when my friend found me the next morning and called nine-nine-nine. The ambulance took me to the hospital and my friend called Chloe. When I finally was able to remember what happened, I told the police and they placed a guard outside my hospital door. Chloe and Tom came over to be with me. I told Chloe what happened but begged her not to tell Tom. I was worried what he would do, he's always been like a big brother to me. We told him I was in a car accident. He didn't know any of this until tonight. I was in the hospital for a couple days and told Chloe and Tom to go home but I would follow as soon as I could travel. The police escorted me onto the ferry at Liverpool and made the crossing with me just to be sure Ben wasn't on the boat. Tom picked me up and I've been here ever since.

"It was two months later when I received the first phone call and text message. I thought he was out of my life for good until that moment. It's been going on for three months now. I accepted a job in Bantry, data-entering, in order to take the threat away from Chloe, Tom and the kids but I don't start for another month. I can't bring Ben here to them. You have no idea. He put a gun to my head that night and told me he would kill every single person I loved. He would always find me and I would watch helplessly as my family was ripped away from me, as he had watched his ripped away from him. He's a maniac. And I don't know what to do."

Emmet had not spoken throughout her speech. He was still quiet when she finished. Mara timed twenty seconds went by before he said a single word.

"What is being done to catch this bastard?" Emmet demanded, his voice low.

"As far as I'm aware, not much," she answered. "The police don't know where he is. They couldn't trace the phone because he keeps changing burners. Honestly, I don't know where he is. All I know is he has my new number."

"Did you give someone, anyone, over there your new number?"

"No."

"Are you absolutely certain? Even your friend who call nine-nine-nine?" Emmet asked.

"No, she knew the risk and didn't want it. I asked the police to let her know I had landed safely. I don't know how he got it," she said. "He must have contacts."

"This man abused you in one of the most horrible ways possible, and now he's stalking you. You need to tell the police. They don't take this lightly, Mara," Emmet's voice caressing her name sent shivers down her spine.

"Would you..." she cleared her throat. "Would you come with me?"

Emmet paused a moment but sighed and continued. "Aye, woman, I'll come with ya."

"Thank you."

Neither of them said anything for a few moments until Emmet began, "well, it's late."

"Wait," she replied hurriedly. "Please."

"What is it?"

"Could... could I buy you a pint?" she asked. "Make up for what I said?"

"Right now? I don't think anything close is open," Emmet said. "It's after three."

"No, not right now, but maybe tomorrow?" she asked. He hesitated. "Please? Let me make it up to you. I'm sorry."

After a moment and a soft resigned sigh, he went on. "You don't need to make anything up to me, but if it'll make you feel better, aye. Maybe my brother Sean or Cabhan can come too."

"Don't want it to look like a date?" she asked.

"No, I don't," he replied without hesitation or inflection. Mara bit her lip to stop the gasp from the hurt she felt at his words.

"All right," she said softly.

They were silent again for a little while until Emmet spoke again, softly. "I'm sorry. Just hearing those words, even though I know they weren't directed at me, hit home. I am not looking for a... relationship."

"One pint, does not a relationship make," she said.

"I know, but it's more the mere implication that I'm..." his voice trailed off and he was quiet for a moment. "Look, this guy needs to be stopped and I'll go with you to the Gardaí but that's as far as it can go. I'm not free now."

"You have a girlfriend?" she asked.

"No, it's not that," he said.

"You're speaking in riddles, Emmet."

"I know," he sighed. "Suffice it to say this? I like you, Mara. I like you a lot and if I didn't have this damn issue hanging like a noose around my neck, I wouldn't hesitate to take you up on that offer of a pint, but I can't. I can be there for you as a friend, but I can't be seen with you or anyone."

"All right," she answered. "I'll take that as a not now but maybe."

"Aye, good," he replied. "Listen, I have a very... physical attraction to you, Mara but there's more to us than us. You are my ex's sister and I am... quite a bit older than you."

"What's not even a decade between adults?" She teased.

"Heh," he breathed. "I want you to know, I'm here if you need me but that's it."

"For now."

"Hopefully," he sighed. "Now, it's late. You need your rest. Call me when you want to go to the police and I'll be there."

"Wait," she called to him. "Could you just... Never mind."

"Could I what?"

"Could you stay on the phone?" she replied. "I feel safe talking to you and it might help me sleep."

There was no answer from him for a beat. Finally, he took a deep breath and answered. "All right."

"Thank you," she whispered.

Burrowing under the sheets and quilts, she turned on her side and brought her knees up to lie in the fetal position. She sighed softly when she heard his breathing and fell asleep with one final thought. She wished she could feel his heat beside her as well as his breathing.

Chapter Eight

Emmet could hear Mara's soft breathing and knew she was asleep but he couldn't bring himself to hang up the phone. It had been a while since he heard the soft sounds of a woman asleep. All his hook ups had been just that, hook up and leave. Once or twice there had been a sleep over, but he wasn't the type unless it was a relationship and his relationships usually didn't last longer than the length of time women were on vacation in Ireland.

Lying in his bed propped up on the pillows, his black Labrador resting beside him, he stroked his dog's head. No matter how much he wanted Mara, he couldn't. He couldn't risk it. Trevor meant more to him than any hookup. Though somehow, he knew Mara would not be just a hookup. His stomach clenched when he thought of possibly having them both with him. Looking around his one-bedroom apartment, his mind wondered at how it would look with a woman's touch. The crossed hurling sticks over his couch would probably be the first things to go and maybe some fresh flowers in that vase he had tucked away from the bouquet he had received when he was laid up in the hospital after a motorcycle crash. At thirty-six, he took pride in keeping his place clean, but it was definitely cold and all male.

Checking his phone when he heard a text message chime in, he put Mara on speaker and checked the message.

Nessie: Did you call her?

Chuckling, he tapped out his reply.

Emmet: Shouldn't you be sleeping?

Nessie: Your nephew is keeping me awake. So, did you?

Emmet: Are you okay? Is Sean there?

Nessie: Of course, but he went to make me a cup of tea. Now stop changing the subject and tell me. Did you call her?

Emmet: Fine, Jaysus woman, yes, I called her. I'm actually still on the phone with her.

Nessie: Then what the hell are you doing talking to me?! Go on, lover boy.

Emmet: She's asleep.

Nessie: ...What? Wore her out already?

Rolling his eyes, he chuckled and tapped out the message.

Emmet: I taught Sean all my moves for "phone calls". You should ask him about it then tell me about how I wore her out.

Nessie: You're horrible. But I'm sure your brother will enjoy the consequences of your last text.

Emmet laughed out right, but immediately froze when he heard Mara moan. When the coast was clear, he typed a response.

Emmet: TMI, babe, but have fun.

When she didn't answer, he clicked over to the phone call. Mara was still asleep and the soft vibrations that shuttered through his phone speaker made him smile. Her cute little snores acted like a lullaby. Plugging the charger into his phone, he set his phone next to his pillow, still on speaker. He lowered his body down and rolled onto his side. The phone stared back at him. He closed his eyes, took a deep breath and let sleep take over, wishing everything would work out and soon.

Mara slowly woke from the best sleep she had in years. Stretching, she looked over and saw her phone sliding down the mattress. Oddly, it was still connected to a call, but her battery was at five percent. Quickly, she plugged it in to the charger and heard Emmet chuckle on the other end.

"Good morning," he said.

Biting her lip, a flash of him entered her mind. Shirtless, sitting up in bed, white sheets draped over his waist, a few days' worth of beard darkening his stern jaw, his light blue eyes heavy with sleep, his auburn hair tousled on the top of his head yet cut close on the sides. She reveled in the shiver that stole up her spine.

"Hello," she whispered back then cleared her throat.

"That was a very sultry hello," Emmet chuckled.

Giggling, she covered her face like a teenager. "It's morning," she defended.

"'Tis," he replied.

"I have no voice in the morning," she explained.

"I'm not complaining."

Knowing he would want to change the subject, she went on. "Were we on the phone the whole night?"

"I would assume so since my phone registers nearly six hours," he said. "And we started the conversation at three."

"I've never... I've never done that before."

"Me neither," he admitted.

"I guess we should hang up then?"

"I guess," he replied. Neither of them did.

"I'm glad you called," she whispered.

"Me too," Emmet stated. Again, they were quiet.

"When can I buy you that pint?" She asked.

He sighed and a shuffle sounded through the speaker as if he ran a hand down his face.

"Whenever we have someone available to go with us," he answered.

"Right," she agreed. After a moment, she tried to stop the words, but they were out of her mouth before she could. "Are you in the middle of a divorce?"

"What?" Emmet questioned. "No."

"Oh, then why?"

"Christ, woman, I just can't," he stated frustrated by calm. "Drop it, Mara, please. I'm asking you to just drop it."

"All right," she answered. "I just want to get to know you better."

"I want that as well, but I can't right now," he said. "Give me... a month. Please."

"It's all right, Emmet," she replied. "I don't understand, but it's okay. I'm used to a guy not telling me things."

"I'm nothing like him," the flash of anger in his words made her close her eyes.

"I'm sorry, that was uncalled for," she apologized. "I don't know if Tom or Chloe will want to go, maybe one of your brothers?"

"I'll see what I can do."

"I should go."

"Me too."

"Thanks for... last night."

"You're welcome."

She didn't want to hang up but when the line went dead, she took a deep breath. He was right. He was her sister's ex and she would never want to put Chloe in that situation, but the childhood crush she had on the man of her dreams, rose its head. Instead of making her feel like the unwanted little sister, he would play with her or talk to her whenever they were all together. She remembered one warm summer day, they all went to the beach and when no one else wanted to go into the water with her, he offered, and they splashed around playing. She was no older than ten and he was nearly nineteen, already over six feet tall, broad and handsome as hell. She fell in love with him then.

A knock at her door drew her attention. She called for them to come in. Chloe opened the door and forced a smile.

"He called?" she asked. Mara nodded. "Good. Listen... I know you're starting to care for him. But I also know there is a lot you don't know about him."

"I know," she answered. "But I'm not, Chlo, honestly. He's your ex. My loyalty is to you."

Chloe looked over her shoulder and stepped inside the room, closing the door behind her. Walking over to the bed, she slowly lowered herself down.

"I would never stand in your way, Mara," she whispered. "I remember how... magnetic he can be. Let me just say there's nothing quite like being in his arms..." she looked down. "Apart from Tom's of course. But he's also hotter than the sun. Stand too close and you'll get burnt. I don't want that for my sister. I... you know what happened between us, I won't rehash it but just know; Emmet is the type of guy who is fun, passionate, and a once in a lifetime experience, but he's also dark and secretive. There's a side of him not many people know. He's always strived to hide it, but there's a darkness in him."

"There's a darkness in me too," Mara said softly. "And I love you, big sister, but you have to let me make my own mistakes."

"You have already made mistakes, Mara," Chloe stated. "Don't make another one."

Mara's face went dark. "What is that supposed to mean?"

"It means use your head," Chloe replied. "Emmet will break your heart. He will leave you worse than Benjamin did. Don't make the same mistake twice."

After staring at her sister and hoping against hope she would retract what she said and blame the pregnancy hormones, she nodded and got out of bed. Grabbing her t-shirt, she pulled it over her sleep camisole and stepped into her skinny jeans.

"Where are you going?" Chloe asked.

"Out, away from you before I say something I'll regret."

"Mara, it's nine in the morning. Use your head."

"You love saying that, don't you?" Mara snapped. "Why don't you use yours? Admit it, the real reason you don't want me with Emmet is because you're still in love with him."

"I am not," Chloe denied.

"You've never been a good liar," she replied. "You can say you love Tom all you wish but it's Emmet you want."

"Absolutely not," she stated. "Tom means more to me than Emmet ever could. I tried to test myself, but as much as I tried to remember the good times, all I could think of was Tom and how much I love him. There was nothing, no feelings, no anger, no love, nothing, except worry for you."

"I don't need your worry."

"Someone has to, you won't worry about yourself."

"Maybe I should leave."

"And go where?" Chloe demanded. "You have no money

and no one to protect you but us."

Mara stopped at the door and turned to look at her sister.

"Better that, than live in fear of you and your reaction to who I date or who I want. If I want Emmet, what will you do? What will Tom do?"

"If you want him fine, have him. He's not mine to give away nor mine to claim. But you'll have to tell Tom."

Mara rolled her eyes and pushed open the door, freezing when she saw Tom on the other side, poised to knock.

"Why is that man's name being mentioned in my home?" Tom demanded lowering his hand.

"Ask your wife," Mara replied sliding out and leaving the room.

"Tommy," Chloe started.

"Tell me, Chlo, I need to know what's going on. Am I never to get away from him?

Mara heard the beginnings of Chloe's explanation and did feel a pang of sorrow for what she said to her sister. But knowing if she stayed to hear Tom's reaction, she would leave anyway, angry. There was no love loss between Tom and Emmet. Mara had seen the hatred from them both. Tom even went so far as to refuse to say Emmet's name. They had been best friends since Mara could remember but after Chloe married him, even before, Tom never wanted to hear Emmet's name. Needing fresh air to clear her head, Mara got into her car and drove, unsure where she was going.

Chapter

Nine

Emmet walked down the stairs of his flat, his black Labrador trotting beside him.

"Ready to go to grandma's and grandpa's, Jacks?" he spoke to his dog. In answer, the lab wagged his tail harder. "Yeah, I know, you love it because they spoil you." Jacks answered him with a soft bark.

He needed a day of riding to get through the mess of thoughts running through his head. His dog was not the needy kind but he didn't feel right leaving him alone in the flat all day. One call to his dad and stepmother and he was on his way to attach the sidecar to his motorcycle. Zipping up his worn leather jacket, he headed out the main door and into the street. Glancing behind him to his favorite view, he stopped mid-step.

Mara's back was to him, but he would know her figure and dark hair anywhere. Jacks looked up at him and then back at the woman, his tail wagging slower. He let out a small yip breaking Emmet out of his thoughts.

"Hold on, lad, we'll be heading out in a minute." Walking away from his dog, he headed over to where she stood, her back still to him, arms wrapped around herself. "Couldn't keep away, hmm?"

She gasped and turned too quickly. Tripping, she screeched and fell into him. Emmet caught her to his chest without so much as a grunt.

"Easy there," he said.

"Sorry," she replied looking up at him and straightening. "You surprised me. What are you doing here?"

"I live over there," he pointed to the building behind them.

"Oh, sorry, you must think I'm stalking you."

"The thought had crossed my mind," he teased. "Why are you here?"

"I had to get away," she answered. "Chloe was... hormonal."

"I am not going to comment," he laughed. "I don't want to earn an elbow in the ribs."

When Mara didn't answer and turned back to the view before them, he looked down at his dog, the old grey and black face questioning.

"What happened?" he asked. "I'm guessing it has to do with me."

"What is it about you, Emmet? Why can't we McGrath women stay away from you?" She asked.

"I wish I knew," he replied. "You McGrath women have always been like a Siren call to me."

"Both of us?" Mara asked. Emmet looked down and away from her searching eyes. "She warned me about you," she finally went on.

"Good," Emmet replied.

"She told me there's a darkness in you. She wanted to tell me more, but I wouldn't let her."

Emmet's heartrate skyrocketed. "What did she want to tell you?"

"I don't know," she shrugged. "But whatever it is, I don't care."

"Mara, you should," he replied. "I'm not a good man. You need to stay away from me."

"You can say that all you want," she said. "But I know the man who used to play with me when I was a kid so I didn't feel left out. I know the man who held me right here and let me cry. I know the man who stayed on the phone with me all night so I could sleep. I know that man and that's the man I want."

"You can't have him," he replied. "He comes with more baggage than anyone should have."

"So do I," she whispered. She didn't say anything for a moment then continued. "While I was driving, I thought about leaving. I thought about driving up to Belfast to take the ferry and cross to Scotland. I thought about going up to the Highlands and disappearing, but I couldn't. I wanted to see you again, but I didn't know where you were. I swung by the dealer and met a man named Paddy. He told me you weren't in today and wouldn't tell me where you lived."

"Paddy is a good friend, but I'm sorry he didn't tell you. I wouldn't have minded."

"No, it's a good thing. He was protecting you. He didn't know if I was some crazy ex-fling or a stalker. I was happy he didn't tell me, made me know you were safe. But then I thought of the place you shared with me." She turned to face him again. "Why do I feel so comfortable and safe with you Emmet?"

"I… have that affect," he whispered.

"Why do I want to kiss you when I know it's wrong?"

"It is wrong, we can't," he replied. "You shouldn't be

here. We can't do this to Chloe."

"I know that, but it doesn't stop the feelings I have for you. I want to know what it's like to kiss you. I always wondered, ever since I saw you and Chloe kissing. I don't want to hurt my sister, but I can't leave you alone. I'm sorry."

His eyes dropped to her lips as they parted in a soft breath that teased his chin. "You don't have to. I don't want to hurt Chloe again but I feel the same. I'm fighting it."

"Me too." Lifting to her toes, she came up to his nose and rose her head higher.

"Mara," he breathed. "Don't."

Ignoring his low warning, she brushed her lips softly against his. He did not respond but when she pulled back slightly, he groaned and pulled her tightly against him. One hand pressed to the small of her back, the other buried in her hair pulling her lips back to his. They crashed together in a frantic dance. She wrapped her arms around his neck and pulled herself up using his body as leverage. Their lips and tongues dueled with each other's, neither gave any quarter. The low hum she gave only fueled his overheated blood.

Then, like a bucket of cold water, he heard the subtle click of a camera lens. Pulling away from her so fast, she stumbled and fell back, landing hard on the stones at their feet. His eyes searched frantically for the cameraman only to see two tourists walking along the water's edge, taking pictures of the mountains beyond.

When he heard Mara's hiss and then a familiar licking sound, he looked down to see Jacks licking her face and Mara rubbing her wrist.

"Oh god, I'm sorry," Emmet said and crouched down to her. "Are you hurt? Jacks, back." He ordered his dog.

"My arse bloody hurts," she started to giggle. "But that's what falling on it twice in two days will do."

He chuckled but pushed a stray strain of hair behind her

ear. "I'm sorry."

"What happened? You went ice cold on me. Am I that bad at kissing?"

"Not at all," he answered.

"Then what caused you to pull away so quickly?"

"Please, that can't happen again," he said.

"You made that clear," she replied, wincing as she stood. "But can you tell me what happened? I don't normally scare a man off after the first kiss."

"Mara, it's not that I don't want you. Christ, I want you, badly. I just—"

"I know," she cut him off gently. "You aren't interested or in a position for a relationship right now. Please be honest with me, Emmet. All I can think of is it's because of my past with Benjamin."

"What?" Emmet demanded. "Christ no!" Turning away from her, he thrust his hands through his hair and took a deep breath. Jacks looked up between them both, then turned to Emmet. Walking over to him, he nudged his leg and whined. Instinctively, Emmet reached down to scratch behind his ears.

Mara stepped forward and placed a gentle hand on his arm. He turned to look at her and hoped she saw the desperation in his eyes.

"It's okay," she whispered. "You don't have to tell me. We hardly know each other and here I'm asking you to confide in me as if a lover."

He finally straightened from petting his dog and she wrapped her arms around him, embracing him, breathing in his leather scent. Slowly, he wrapped his arms around her and rested his chin on her head.

"I have a son," he admitted softly. Mara pulled back gently and looked up at him. "His name is Trevor. He's three," he went on. "I never knew about him. His mother was American and a... vacation fling but I got a letter from her a couple months back telling me about him. But before I could see her, she had died of a terminal disease. She expressed a desire I take custody, but her parents are fighting it. They're labeling me a player. Saying I have no desire to raise a child. My solicitor says I have a case because I am the lad's biological father and his mother never told me. She also named me his guardian in her will. But he advised me to stay away from any woman not related by blood or marriage, not to give them any more to use against me. They're going to paint me as a drunk philanderer and they may succeed, like. I offered to settle, give me custody and I will give them any say in how I raise him, but they want full and will never let me see my boy." His voice cracked.

"They'll take him back to America. I never thought I wanted to be a father, but I met him when they received the summons from my solicitor. He knew I was his father. When he called me *daddy,* I immediately knew I had to do everything I could to be his father. When I held him in my arms, I fell in love with him. He's my son. I never could let him go. So please understand, it's not you. Jaysus, I would have you in my bed already if it weren't for him. When we kissed, Christ, I wanted more, but then I heard a camera lens shutter and I thought maybe they have had me followed. I'm sorry I hurt you. I seem to be good at that."

"Emmet," she breathed. It was strange how in that moment he changed to her. He was no longer the bad boy fling she always thought he could be. He was a father and was putting his child's care above everything. Something deeply feminine reared its head within her and as she looked into his dark blue eyes, she fell deeper in love with him. Reaching out, she pushed a piece of his auburn hair away from his eyes. "I care about you more than I probably should, and I don't know why. But I will keep my distance from you until you are free. I would never want to stand in the way of you getting everything you desire."

"I care about you too, Mara. God help me but I do," he replied. "I think I always have ever since I found you in the ditch with a broken ankle and your bike on top of you."

Mara's brows furrowed but flashes of memories came back to her. She was eight and had a fight with Chloe. She took her bike and rode down the back pasture but lost control and flipped over, crashing down a hill. She remembered the pain and lying there crying for help, when she heard a scooter pull up. Flashes of a young Emmet, no more than sixteen sliding down the incline to her, his voice soft and soothing as he asked who she was and where she lived. She remembered him taking her into his arms and carrying her all the way. The soft musky smell of his leather coat grounded her. It was the only time in her life she felt safe.

"I wondered why this scent was so familiar and comforting," she took a deep sniff.

"Are you sniffing me?" Emmet chuckled.

"Maybe," she grinned. "My knight in shining armor on his great white steed."

"More like a teenager in ripped jeans and a moped scooter," he replied. "But I always watched out for you."

She reached up to kiss him softly but pulled back before they regretted it.

"I will wait for you," she promised.

"I don't know how long it will be."

"I would wait another twenty years for you if I had to."

"I come with a packaged deal," he explained. "If I get custody, I'll have a son to think about. Could you handle an instant family? Being an instant mother?"

"It would be an honor to be with you and Trevor."

"What about Chloe?" he asked. "I'm under no delusion I broke her heart. I don't know how she'll feel."

"Right now, don't think of anyone but your son."

Taking a deep breath, he nodded. "I'm… scared."

Tears pricked the back of Mara's eyes as she wrapped her arms around him, holding him tightly.

"Then it's my turn to be here for you," she whispered. They held each other for a long time until Jacks whined again, and Emmet turned to look at the old face staring back at him.

"I should get Jacks to my parents," he whispered.

"Okay," she answered. "I'm going to stay here for a little longer. I don't want to go back yet."

"Another fight with Chloe?"

"I always leave, I know," she sighed. "But this time, I don't want to go back. We both said things and I can't face it."

"Come with me then," he said.

"I thought you weren't able to be seen with me," she replied.

"I know, but I can't leave you alone. I'm dropping Jacks off and I was going to hit the road. I needed a long drive, clear my head. Come with me."

"Are you sure?"

"Aye, I am," he answered.

"I would love to."

"Good," Emmet grinned and offered his arm to her. They walked to his motorcycle, Jacks jumped into the sidecar and watched them as Emmet helped her put her helmet on and kicked the motorcycle into gear. Mara wrapped her arms around his middle as he zipped up his leather jacket and buckled his helmet. "All set?" she nodded. "Hang on then." He eased out so no to jostle Jacks in the side car but soon they were on the road to his parent's house.

Pulling up to the cottage, Emmet noticed his father's shed door was closed but Sinéad's car was not there. His sister had moved back home after her year abroad in Australia. Pulling off his helmet, he untied Jacks' leash and helped the old pup out. Detaching the sidecar, he set it aside. Mara stayed seated on the motorcycle and took off her helmet, shaking out her dark hair.

"Should I stay here?" she asked.

"Don't take this wrong, but yeah," he replied. "I know my ma. She'll rope us both in to having breakfast and to tell her all about us. Personally, I want to get on the road."

"Say no more," she grinned and put her helmet back on. Emmet winked and walked Jacks up the steps to his parent's one-story house.

Knocking then opening the door, he called out. "Ma? Da'?"

"In the kitchen, Em," his father's voice rang out. Jacks barked excitedly and bounded off, Emmet following behind.

Hearing his parents greet his lab, he smiled fondly. Jacks was like a puppy again whenever he went to visit his grandparents. When he turned the corner, he saw his step-mother who was more like a mother to him, turn down the gas on the stove. Greeting him with a big smile, she stepped around her husband, who was petting Jacks and threw her arms around him.

"How are you, darling?" she hugged him tightly. "Are you hungry? I have some fresh scones ready."

"Oh ma," he sighed. "You would use scones against me."

She grinned conspiratorially and patted his cheek. "You've lost weight, darling, you need to eat."

"I have plenty of weight believe me. I love your scones but today I just want to get on the road. Thanks for looking after Jacks for me," he said turning to head to the door.

"Wait, will you at least let me pack you a couple?" she

asked. "I've made too many and if you don't eat some, Orin will eat them all," she looked pointedly at his father still playing with Jacks.

"It's not my fault, woman, you make them too damn good," he said.

"I can't, I don't know when I'll stop off to eat them. I should get going," Emmet replied.

"What's the hurry?" Orin asked standing. "Stay a minute longer, have a scone and let's talk."

"I really can't," he answered, looking toward the door.

"Has something happened?" Dierdre asked.

"What do you mean?" Emmet replied.

"Is everything okay with Trevor?" she questioned.

Emmet looked away. When Trevor's mother first approached him, he had been so shell-shocked he had told his family everything but after receiving the letter the other day he wasn't sure he could tell them the truth. He didn't want them to get their hopes up.

"I just really want to hit the road," Emmet sidestepped.

"All right, love," Dierdre acquiesced. "Be careful. Whatever it is, you know you can tell us, right?"

"Aye, aye," he waved them off. "Thank you for taking care of Jacks." Turning to look at his pup, he crouched down. "Be good, lad. I'll see you tonight."

"Will you be here for dinner?" Orin asked.

"Probably not," he answered. "I should swing by around nine, if that's all right."

"Let him stay the night," Orin offered. "We'll see you tomorrow at Sean's and Ness's to help them with the baby's room. I could use your help with a couple things there too."

"Aye? Cheers," he thanked his father. "I'll leave the sidecar here. Do you think you could take it to Sean's?"

"Aye, no worries."

"I have an appointment at ten tomorrow morning, but I'll be by after that. Anything needed I could pick up for tomorrow?" Emmet offered.

"I don't think so, love," Deirdre replied.

"Let me know. I'd be happy to."

"Cheers, lad, be careful," Orin told him and was about to walk him to the door when Emmet got there first and quickly shut it after him.

"Everything all right?" Mara asked as she saw him walk quickly out of the house.

"Yeah, let's go," he said and pulled on his helmet. Straddling his motorcycle, he kicked it into gear. Mara wrapped her arms around his waist, and they pulled back onto the road.

Chapter Ten

Orin looked back at his wife as they stood at the window to see Emmet walk back to his bike.

"So *that's* why he was so anxious to leave," Orin said.

"Who is she?" Deirdre asked.

"No idea."

"He needs to be careful."

"Why do you think she kept her helmet on and didn't come in?"

"He didn't want to introduce us," the sadness in his wife's voice made Orin turn and pull her into his arms.

"I'm sure that's not it, love," he replied, kissing her hair. "He's an odd one that one. But he loves us. He's working his life out right now. He got news no one would be prepared for."

"He hasn't gotten the DNA test back yet, do you think?"

"Not sure, he seemed different when we asked about

him," Orin stated. "But come now, love, he probably doesn't want us to get our hopes up for another grandchild."

"True, but I would love that boy even if he wasn't Emmet's. He needs family."

"You haven't met him yet, love," Orin teased.

"It's not hard to know a child needs love after his mother dies when he's so young."

Orin kissed her hair again and looked down at her. "I love you, ya daft woman."

"I love you, ya wee bully," she teased and kissed him gently. "Now, my scones are going to waste."

"They'll never go to waste while I'm here, love," he replied taking her hand and letting her lead him to the table where Jacks waited patiently for his meal.

After a visit to the local Gardaí station, Emmet and Mara rode for hours until Emmet pulled up to a pub and kicked the stand of his motorcycle. Turning it off, he sat back. Removing his helmet, he turned to Mara who hadn't let go of him yet. Chuckling, he turned in his seat and lifted her tinted visor.

"First motorcycle ride?" he asked.

She nodded quickly. "Those mountain roads I didn't like but holding on to you made it better." She gave him a gentle squeeze.

Grinning, he teasingly flicked her visor down and stood beside his bike. "Come on," he said. She pulled off her helmet and looked up at him.

"No one is around, I looked before I removed my helmet." She reached up and kissed his cheek. "Now, I'm starving. Where are we?"

"Limerick, or there abouts," Emmet replied. "I always

drive up this way. My parents have a cottage in Sligo. I head there occasionally when they don't have it rented. It's a beautiful place. But don't worry, we won't be going that far."

"I wouldn't mind," she shrugged biting her lower lip. "What are we doing here?"

"Well, I haven't had breakfast," he stated. "And it's well past lunch."

"By all means, O'Quinn," she teased. "Don't let me stand in the way of a growing man and his breakfast."

"Damn right," he grinned, patting his flat stomach. "The pubkeeper knows me here though, so..."

"Got it," she replied. "Thanks for letting me tag along... cousin."

He nodded slowly and opened the door for her. "My pleasure."

"Afternoon, Em," the pubkeeper called.

"Hiya, Seamus," Emmet answered. "How goes it?"

"Grand," he replied. "Out for a ride?"

"Aye, it's a lovely day," he said.

"'Tis," he agreed. "And lovely company."

"This is Mara," Emmet introduced.

"His cousin," she stepped forward.

"Aye, my ma's sister's kid," he said. "She's been away for a few years just showing her the area."

"I didn't know Donna had kids," he stated surprised.

"No," Emmet chuckled. "My birth mother." He ignored the subtle glance Mara gave him.

"Ah, I see."

"He's showing me what's changed since I've been away, like," Mara elaborated.

"That can't be much," Seamus replied smiling. "Haven't seen you around afore, lass."

"I grew up in Monaghan," she explained.

"Well, what can I get ya?" he asked.

"Mine's a pint of my usual please, Seamus, thanks, and the special," Emmet replied.

"I'll have the same," Mara stated.

The pubkeeper went back to the kitchen to give their orders to the chef. The only other ones in the pub were two older men and an Irish wolfhound lounging in the sunlight that streamed through the window.

"Sit or do you fancy a game of darts?" Emmet asked.

Her eyes went to the pool table in the corner. "I'd prefer pool."

"Ah, well just so you know," he walked over to the table and picked up the pool stick, twirling it for good measure. "I am known at my local as the master."

"Oh?" she asked. "I don't know if I'm *that* good. But I look forward to it."

Emmet had pulled off his jacket two games and three pints ago. Mara was up two to one and the one was only because her elbow was jarred by a passing patron. He thanked his friend silently as it helped him win.

The pub had gradually gotten busier as the hours ticked by and sweat dripped down his forehead. To distract him, Mara had stripped out of her shirt, down to the camisole she had on underneath. Leaning over the pool table, she provided enough distraction for him and every other man in the pub. Standing at the head of the table chalking her cue, she watched him as he contemplated his next move. She had him in a corner and he knew it. Taking a draw on her local amber brew, she watched him line up, then shake his head and walk around the table.

"It should be illegal, you know," he said.

"What?" she feigned innocence.

"Oh, don't give me that," he grumbled. "You're giving my reputation a run for its money, so you are."

"I'm merely playing the game," she teased. "So grateful to be learning from the pool master."

He lined up at the foot of the table and teased the cue a couple times. Stretching, she took a deep breath and rolled her shoulders successfully causing him, and every other male patron, to look up at her. The cue slipped from his hand and the cue ball hit the striped ball too softly, rolling away from the pocket.

"Tsk," she sighed. "Bad luck."

He narrowed his eyes at her as she stared at him and slowly drained her beer. Sauntering over, he watched, a slight smirk toying the corner of his mouth. She slipped between him and the table.

"Excuse me," her breathy voice raked down his spine. "I have to sink the eight ball in the side pocket and win."

He stepped back and watched as she lined up her cue. Bending over, she made sure her best attribute was on display for him and Emmet didn't fail to notice.

Teasing the cue, she glanced back at him over her shoulder. His eyes were exactly where she wanted them. Looking back at the table, she struck the cue ball which knocked the eight ball into the side pocket right where she wanted it.

She straightened and turned back to him. His eyes trailed up to hers as she stepped closer. Reaching around him, she grabbed his beer and took a sip, never breaking eye contact.

"My game I believe," she finally said.

"Aye," he whispered. "I'll rack them up?"

"For others, I think you've lost enough for one day, don't you?" she asked.

Taking his pint, she walked over to their food and sat down. He watched her, unable to move as too many emotions flooded his veins. She raised her eyes up to his.

"Are you going to join me... cousin?" she questioned.

Shaking himself out of his stupor, he walked to their table and sat down. Motioning to Seamus for another pint, he leaned in close.

"Enjoying yourself?" he asked.

"Immensely," she replied. "It was such a pleasure learning from you... pool master."

His eyes narrowed at her as she grinned. "Minx," he said just as Seamus handed him his pint.

"And proud of it, thank you," she replied. "Just be thankful I didn't bet you anything."

"I am sure I would be broke by now."

She looked up at him with a look that stopped him mid-drink. "Who said anything about money?"

Emmet choked on the beer he was drinking. Coughing and sputtering, he grabbed the napkins on the table to cover his mouth as he eyed her.

"Oh, Emmet!" she cried innocently. "Are you all right?" His gazed narrowed on her and she answered by flashing a brilliant grin. "There now, no harm done, cuz." Settling, she took another bite. "This is very good," she said.

"Mmhmm," he replied, keeping his head down as he ate. "How's the car?" he finally asked.

"Hadn't had much chance to drive it," she admitted. "But from the little I have it's very... satisfactory."

"Damn," he breathed. "Well good, it if gives you any trouble, you just let me know."

"Oh, don't worry," she locked eyes with him. "I know just who to take it to for something so... delicate."

Emmet tossed back his beer and finished his food quickly. "Another game?"

"Aren't you beat enough, O'Quinn?" she asked tapping the top of the beer glass, eyeing him. "There's a fine line between pleasure and pain."

"I never back down from a challenge," he answered.

"Oh good," she replied, her eyes on his again. "But how about a raincheck. There's so much more to see."

"True."

"Take me to a place you love."

"Right," he replied. "I'll just settle up and meet you outside."

"I'm looking forward to it," she replied, hopping down off the high seat and sauntering to the door, pulling her shirt on over her camisole.

As Mara waited for Emmet to settle their bill, she stood beside the motorcycle and dug her phone out of her pocket. Chloe had called her twice and sent her three texts. As she was about to type out a message to her sister, the phone rang again. Sighing, she answered it and put it to her ear.

"Hello?" She said.

"Oh, thank god," Chloe's voice sighed on the other end. "Mara, I'm sorry about what I said. It's these damn hormones, that's not an excuse but I am sorry."

"I'm sorry too, Chlo. Really. I didn't mean what I said about you loving Emmet more than Tom. It was a low blow and I said it to hurt you. I'm sorry."

"Truce?" Chloe asked.

"Truce. You know we swore we'd never let a man come between us. I guess neither of us thought it would be Emmet O'Quinn."

"He hasn't come between us, Mar," Chloe assured. "I did love him and yes, he hurt me, but he and I were not mean to be. I love Tommy. More than life and I'll be forever grateful to Emmet for introducing us. When I was with him, there was always something missing. I was a kid and didn't know any better but now I know what true love is and that's what was missing with Emmet. I would never stand in his way, nor yours to be able to find that sort of love yourselves. I told Tom everything and while he's not happy about Emmet, we back you. We support you. We love you."

"Thank you, Chloe," she answered. "I love you both too."

"Are you okay? Where are you?" She asked.

"Somewhere near Limerick," she revealed. "I don't know, we just drove."

"Are you with Emmet?"

"Yes."

"All right, I won't keep you. I just wanted to make sure you're okay. I tried calling him earlier just to see but he didn't answer. Just be careful. Will you be back tonight?"

"I don't know," she answered. "I don't know where we're going right now."

"Please just text me if you won't be home," Chloe asked. "No judgement, just want to make sure you're safe."

"Thank you," she answered. "And I'll text you."

"I love you, little sister."

"I love you, too. Are you sure you're okay with this?"

"I'll not lie, knowing you are with him... or will be..."

"You mean sleep with him?"

"Yes," Chloe stated. "It's difficult for me. Emmet was all I knew until Tom. I don't care who you are with but I know what I went through emotionally with him and I don't want to see you get hurt. But I will tell you this, when you bask in his love, he is the sweetest, most caring, commanding and incredible lover. It can consume you. Just promise me, you'll be careful."

"I will," Mara promised. "He's changed, Chloe. There's a reason but I can't tell you. He's not the teen nor early twenties boy you knew. He's grown up."

"I'm glad. Deep down, I know he never meant to hurt me, nor I him and believe me, I have. But if he is your choice, I support you."

"That's very... forgiving of you."

"Oh, mark my words, he hurts you and it's not Tom he has to worry about."

Mara giggled. "Easy there, mama bear."

Chloe laughed too but Mara saw Emmet leave the pub, told her sister she loved her and had to go, then hung up.

Emmet walk out of the pub, checking his phone. "Do you know why Chloe called me?" Emmet asked looking up from his phone.

"She wanted to know where I was," she explained. "I just spoke to her."

"She thought you were with me?"

"She figured after the disagreement we had earlier," she reminded him.

"Disagreement.... about me," Emmet stated. She nodded. Taking a deep breath, he thrust his phone back into his pocket and locked eyes with her.

"She backs me," Mara said. "She and Tom talked. They're okay with this. "

"It doesn't matter, I should take you back. She's right about me. There are things you don't know about me and I feel like I'm cheating you by pretending I'm a good guy."

"Then tell me," Mara said. "It can't be worse than sleeping with a married man."

"You didn't know what you were doing was wrong, I did," Emmet confided.

"Hey," she stepped forward and cupped his jaw. "It's okay. Whatever it is, it's okay." After a beat, she changed the subject. "Now where are you going to take me next?"

Emmet sighed. "Where do you want to go?"

"Take me somewhere that means something to you."

He nodded and pulled on his helmet then straddled his motorcycle. "Get on," he said. "I'm going to show you heaven."

Benjamin couldn't believe his eyes. Mara flaunting herself to the Irish Rogue. He was handsome, Benjamin appreciated men's physiques as much as women's, but Mara was his. Redhead could not have her. If he laid a finger on her, Benjamin would make him suffer. He just had to find his weakness. Sitting in the far corner of the pub, he watched as they played pool. She stripped out of her shirt allowing every man in the pub to ogle her. His hand clenched around the pint glass. Listening to her breathy tone, seeing her bending over putting her arse in the air showing off, Benjamin knew she was a whore, but had never seen it outside the bedroom. The thought of other men touching her, it made him sick. He felt tainted. Maybe it was time to let her go and only make her suffer instead of making her his again. God only knew where it had been and how many diseases she carried. He shuddered and gagged.

"Yes, time to let the whore go. But Red," he shook his head. "Red and I will have fun. I'll find out what you hold most dear and I'll strip it from you just like Mara stripped me of my family."

Leaving when he saw them finishing up, he sat in his rental car and waited. He adjusted the rearview mirror to see

Emmet and Mara swing onto the motorcycle. "What makes you tick? Whatever it is, I hope you're ready to give it up."

Ducking down as they passed him on the road, Benjamin followed at a distance. No need to draw suspicion yet. Simply gather information. Maybe they'll stop off at another pub. He was sure his ball cap and beard wouldn't be enough to disguise himself from Mara, but it was enough to keep her guessing and looking over her shoulder. Grinning as they took a mountain road, Benjamin pulled off to wait for them. The mountain road was deserted, and he didn't want to draw undue attention. He couldn't help the rush of excitement in his veins. The woman had it coming and he couldn't wait to see her face when she realized her world would never be the same.

CHAPTER ELEVEN

Pulling off the road, Emmet maneuvered the bike up the winding path of a narrow mountain road. After a couple heart stopping moments, Mara felt the road level out and looked over his shoulder to see the view. The sea spread out before her, dotted with smaller islands and boats. The sky was blue and, though they were above sea level, the wind was not as blustery as she expected. Parking, Emmet took off his helmet, stood beside the bike and offered his hand to her. They walked together to a half wall which Emmet climbed over carefully and sat, his legs dangling down the rock face. Mara followed and sat beside him.

Neither said anything and in the silence, they listened to the sea and wind sing their song. No one was around, it was their own private paradise. Heaven, just as he said. A single tear slipped down her cheek, but she let the wind blow it from her face. Soon it was followed by another, then another.

"Hey," Emmet said softly. "What's wrong?"

Shaking her head, she wiped the tears. "It's just so

beautiful. I love it here... with you, but I've made such a mess of my life. My one wish would be to go back in time and change it all. Never go to London, never meet Benjamin, never..."

"Never what?" he prompted when she didn't continue.

"Never leave here and you," she replied looking up into his pale blue eyes. "I know we've only known each other as adults for a short time, and I know you are my sister's ex-fiancé, but I just can't shake this feeling I have for you, Emmet. I don't know what it is, but I love being around you. I feel safe with you and I can't tell you the last time I smiled or cared about a man without thinking he wanted something in return. You are a special person and I would be a fool to let our history, your history with my family, take the forefront. I care so much about you. I've thought about you over the years and wondered what you have done with your life. The moment you told me you were a father and how you were willing to put your own thoughts and desires ahead of everything else but the happiness of your son, called to something deep within me and I can't shake the feeling something wonderful is staring me in the face and that is you."

"Mara," he breathed. She grasped the back of his neck and pulled his lips to hers. When he pulled back, he continued speaking. "I never meant to hurt Chloe or you, or any woman I know. I realize now how much of a player I have been, but I have never been more tempted to put life on hold to be with someone, as I am with you."

"I want you, Emmet, god help me, but I do," she confided. "And more than just a lover. I want to know you. I want to know who you are and what you want in life."

"I want you, too," he replied. "But I can't right now. As much as it's killing me, I can't."

"I know," she answered and with one last soft kiss, she pulled back. "I am going to wait for you. No matter what happens. I am here and I'm not going anywhere."

"Bloody hell," he breathed and pulled away from her, thrusting his hands through his hair. "Do you have any idea how much I want you right now?"

"I have a fairly good idea," she nodded.

"If I didn't have this damn thing hanging over me, there would be no question."

"I know."

"I have a meeting with my solicitor tomorrow morning," he went on. "I'm going to tell him about you and see if we can't figure something out. It's not fair."

"No, it's not," she agreed. "But for now, leave it be. Chloe backs me with this but I'm not sure about Tom. She says he does but you both have such a volatile relationship, I could not ask either of you to put your dislike on hold. Tom means a lot to me and I love him like a brother, but I don't want to hurt him or you. I don't want to be the cause of you losing something as important as your son. For now, Emmet, leave it be."

"There's more about me you need to know," he said.

Pressing a finger to his lips, she silenced him. "Don't," she replied. "Don't pressure yourself into telling me something you're not ready to tell me."

Letting out a breath, he nodded. "If someone... Tom... tells you something about me, please don't immediately think the worst of me, no matter what it is. Ask me and give me a chance to explain. There are some things in my past I would rather leave buried but I am certain they're going to come to light, especially with the custody hearing."

"I promise you, Emmet, if something happens, I will speak with you first before passing judgement. I could never judge anyone anyway, not with my past."

"Thank you," he said softly.

"Now," she went on. "I want to stay here for a while just watching the sunset." She rested her head on Emmet's shoulder and they fell silent watching the fading light dance on the crystal waters.

Feeling her head resting between his shoulder blades, Emmet expertly maneuvered his bike down the mountain road and onto a straight path. Dusk had descended and as he drove down the M18, Mara's arms tightened around him. It was nearly dark when he pulled up to a pub in Killarney. When he parked the motorcycle and took off his helmet, he turned in the seat. Mara hadn't let go yet.

"Hey," he breathed when he felt her shake against him. "What's wrong?"

She shook her head but didn't look up at him.

"Mara," he pulled her arms off him and stood. Taking her hands in his, he made her stand with him. Removing her helmet, he gently turned her chin to look at him. "What's wrong? Are you all right? Did I frighten you? I know driving down the M18 on a motorcycle is scary the first time. I'm sorry. I didn't think, I do it all the time."

"No, it's not that," she finally said. He saw the streaks of tears running down her cheeks. "Today was so perfect."

"Then why are you crying?" he asked softly, wiping her tears away.

"Because," she started. "I know it has to end and I don't want it to."

"It doesn't have to."

"It does," she countered. "Your son is more important."

"Hey," he breathed and gently cupped her chin. "Don't shut us out. Let me talk to my solicitor tomorrow. Who knows what he'll say."

"And if he says to leave me be? You have to," she replied. "No matter what."

"I don't think I can."

"You have to, Emmet," she stressed. "Now," she gathered her strength and looked around. "Where are we?"

"Don't tell me you've forgotten Killarney?" He replied taking the cue from her to stop talking about the preverbal elephant in the room.

"It's been a very long time and it's dark out," she answered turning in his arms and looking around. He wrapped his arms around her waist and rested his chin on her head. "Didn't you used to work there?" she asked pointing to Killarney Plaza Hotel.

"I did," he replied. "I was coming back from my first day on the job when I found you crashed in the ditch. But we're not spending the night there, sorry love."

She breathed a laugh. "Pity." Reaching up, she cupped his jaw. "What are we doing here then?"

"Dinner," he replied.

"Have we really spent all day together?" she asked.

"Aye we have," he stated. "It's nearly eight. Don't worry, I'll be a gentleman and get you home before your reputation is affected."

"And if I don't want you to be a gentleman?" she asked rubbing her back against him.

"Heh," he breathed and took a step back. "I won't always be a gentleman around you, but for now, I will be."

"Very well, O'Quinn," she answered, then continued. "Will you do me the honor of escorting me into this public house for nourishment? I find I am famished and in need of sustenance."

"Ever use that English accent again and I'll take you over my knee," he growled.

"Was that supposed to be a dissuasion?" she asked.

Emmet's eyes flashed with something she had never seen. They darkened and he took a step closer. "You play with fire, lass."

"I don't mind getting burnt," she grinned.

Letting out a chuckle, he shook his head. "Let's go," he said. "Before I call in a favor of every one of my friends at the Plaza."

"Again... was that supposed to be a dissuasion?"

"Christ, Mara," he laughed then pulled her into him and pressed his lips to hers. "Stop torturing me."

Patting his cheek, she turned away from him and sashayed into the pub. Watching as she walked, he sighed and stuffed his hands into his pockets. It was going to be a long evening.

Chapter
Twelve

The pub was crowded. The straight design with a long walkway from the front to the back with the bar to the left and seating to the right, made it difficult to walk through but Mara found a two-seat table at the raised dining area, near the middle of the pub. Live music played, the band stationed in the front corner of the entry. The four older men sat together in a small circle, playing an Irish jig. Mara caught all different accents and languages from the people around her, clearly tourists favored the location as well as locals and Mara could see why. The whole place was the perfect embodiment of an Irish Pub.

Emmet went to the bar and ordered for them, then carried their drinks back. They couldn't carry on a conversation due to the noise, so they simply enjoyed the music and drinks while they waited for the food. Catching Emmet watching her, she smiled broadly and took his hand beneath the table. He gave it a small squeeze but dropped it sooner than she wanted when their food finally arrived. Taking in the crowd around them, she reveled in a freedom she hadn't felt before. She was safe, she was happy and she was enjoying herself. When they finished their sandwiches, she leaned back against the wall behind them and Emmet went to the bar to get another round.

As soon as he returned, the leader of the band stood and everyone quieted down.

"Do we have any singers in the room tonight?" a general cheer went up. "Grand! Anyone want to try their hand at a little Irish karaoke?"

Some of the more drunk patrons cheered and stood in line. They endured drunken versions of *Danny Boy* and *Rocky Road to Dublin*. Finally, Emmet leaned over to her and spoke close to her ear.

"You should go up there," he said. "You're a singer, aye?"

"Oh god no," she shook her head. "I'm not drunk enough."

"No need to be. You have actual talent."

"You've never heard me sing."

"I can guess."

"I can't, Emmet."

"Why not?"

"I'm... nervous."

"You wanted to be a professional singer, aye? Now's your chance to see if you really want to pursue that career. Get up there and sing something.... For me."

She sighed harshly. "You would say that, wouldn't you?"

He grinned over the rim of his beer. She took a deep gulp of her Guinness, stood, squared her shoulders and nodded once. "Right. This is your fault, O'Quinn."

She felt Emmet's eyes on her as she stepped down the two steps and walked to the line of people waiting for their turn.

Her stomach was in knots, but she wanted to sing for him. The question was, what would he like to hear? She should have asked him what he liked before she walked away but her nerves got the better of her. Finally, she was next and the man in front of her was finishing up *When Irish Eyes are Smiling.*

Just as the leader waved her forward, she decided which song she wanted to sing. Telling the leader, his eyes grew wide, seeing she was completely serious and not one of the drunk singers. He agreed and told his bandmates.

As the first strain of notes began on the pennywhistle, Mara took a deep breath and began to sing; *She Moved Thru' the Fair.* The key was high, but she was able to sing it. The pub quieted down and stared at her. Her eyes scanned the room but landed on Emmet. The soft look and smile on his face was enough to give her the strength to sing the whole piece. Her eyes left his only a short time, but he grounded her and her nerves were gone. The band backed her up perfectly and was not too overpowering.

The last note drifted through the pub and everyone stayed quiet for a long moment. Mara took a deep breath and waited. Finally, the pub's patrons burst into applause and cheers, Emmet was the loudest one. Giving an awkward curtesy, Mara turned to the band and thanked them, laughing when the leader asked her to sing another. But when the cheers grew raucous demanding another, she blushed and agreed. Since she had sung a ballad, she decided on something more upbeat. *Níl Sé'n Lá* was one of her favorites.

Thankfully, the song got the patrons cheering and drinking. Mara took a sweeping, teasing bow afterward and bounded up the steps to Emmet who swept her up into his arms and planted a firm kiss on her lips.

"That was amazing," he breathed. "You are amazing."

"I couldn't agree more," a man's voice drew their attention. A sandy blonde-haired man with keen brown eyes stood at the railing of the raised section. He walked around and took the two steps up to them. "Is there somewhere we can speak privately?"

"I'm sorry?" Mara asked.

"We were just leaving, actually," Emmet's arm tightened around her waist.

"I'm sorry, where are my manners?" the man smiled and breathed a laugh. "Strange man walks up to you after you sing at a pub and he asks for a moment alone. I can see how it looks. My apologies." He pulled out a business card. "My name is Connor Townsend. I'm a talent scout for Hibernia Talent Agency located in Dublin. I'm here visiting my sister and we came out tonight. I am very glad we did. You said your name was Mara?"

Mara nodded. "Mara McGrath."

"I am pleased to meet you Ms. McGrath. I would very much like to speak with you about possible representation. My firm is looking for the next Irish group, a man and woman duet. I think you would be an excellent candidate. How you sang both a ballad and a jig shows true talent and diversity. I know you said you were just leaving, please take my card and give me a call. I would very much like to present you to my firm."

Mara stared at the card and said nothing until Emmet's hand on her hip squeezed gently. "Thank you," she stumbled around her own feelings. "Mr. Townsend."

"Connor, please."

"Connor, thank you. I will definitely consider it."

"Strongly," Emmet provided.

"Excellent. I'll get back to my sister, but I want to say, I am very excited about the possibility of representing you. You could be the next Celtic sensation," the scout said. "I thoroughly enjoyed your performance. Ms. McGrath," he extended his hand which Mara took, then extended it to Emmet. "Mr. McGrath," he said.

"O'Quinn, we're not married," Emmet replied.

"Apologies again," Connor answered but, to his credit, did not fall into Emmet's trap of looking at Mara differently, as if she were free for him. When another man waved to him at the bar, he nodded. "I'm needed back, there's only so much my partner can handle from my sister asking him when we're going to make us official," he chuckled. "She thinks just because we work together all the time we're a couple. My girlfriend hates it. I hope to speak to you soon, Mara."

"Yes, absolutely. Thank you," Mara said.

"My pleasure," he smiled at them both and left the platform, making his way through the crowd, back to his party.

Mara's dancing eyes turned to Emmet and he took her hand leading her outside and away from the deafening noise of someone else singing. As soon as they were outside, Mara squealed and jumped into his arms. He held her tightly and spun her around.

"Oh my god oh my god oh my god oh my god. Oh my *god!*" she squealed. Emmet set her down and she stared down at the business card as if it was a long-lost treasure.

"Another step closer to your dream," Emmet said.

"Thanks to you," she answered. "You took us here, you encouraged me to sing. If you're not careful, I may think you're my lucky charm and I won't let you go."

"You don't have to let me go," he replied taking her hand and kissing her knuckles.

"Thank you, thank you so much!"

"You sang, love."

"But you believed in me enough to encourage me to. I can't thank you enough."

"I figure a few more of your kisses and I'll be well paid for my part," he winked.

"You can always expect kisses from me, O'Quinn."

"I'm glad." Taking her hand, he paused for a moment. "It's pretty late, let's get you home."

Mara nodded and followed him to the bike, being sure to tuck Mr. Townsend's card away in a safe place.

CHAPTER
THIRTEEN

Emmet pulled up to Chloe's and Tom's house at midnight. The lights were still on indicating someone was still awake inside. When Emmet cut the engine, Mara took off her helmet and swung off the bike.

"Probably Tom," she said, answering the unspoken question in his eyes. Emmet nodded, lowered the kickstand with a single flick of his heel and sat back. Pulling off his helmet, he looked at her. "What? Do I have something on my face?"

"No," he put her mind at ease. "I was just... staring at you."

She smiled slightly, her excitement still showing around her eyes. "Do you want to come in?"

"I do, but I probably shouldn't," he said. "Tom isn't exactly my number one fan."

"They'll have to get used to this... to us," she replied.

"Still," he answered. "Let's ease them into this? There's

more in our past than you know."

"I know I was a kid, but we're both adults now," she stated. "I know I'm not my sister. But I hope you'll see me for me and not the kid you once knew."

"It's both honestly," he replied. "But I don't ever want you to think I look at you as your sister. What was between Chloe and me is in the past. Far in the past. I care about her as someone cares about another person they spent any length of time with. Tom is another story."

"I remember hearing you guys got into a fight," she said.

"We did and I'm not sure he's over that he lost," he answered.

"Did he?" She questioned. "He got the girl in the end."

Emmet said nothing and indicated the door. "You should get inside."

She nodded and turned to go. Just a couple steps toward the front door, she stopped and rushed back to him. Throwing her arms around his neck, she kissed the line where his chin met his jaw, feeling the prickly stubble from a few days of not shaving.

"Thank you for today," she whispered.

"You are very welcome," he answered. "And congratulations. I can't wait to hear what the talent scout has to say."

Pulling back, she locked eyes with him. "You'll be the first to hear... Will I see you again?"

"Soon, I promise," he replied. "I'll call you."

"Text is easier," she said with a glance back at the house. Emmet nodded and took her hand in his, kissed the back, and squeezed her fingers.

"I enjoyed today. Thank you for understanding about Trevor."

"He's a lucky kid to have you as his da'," she said. "Be careful going home."

"I will," he promised. "Get inside, it's bloody freezing out here."

Before she said anything more, she kissed his lips quickly and raced to the stoop. Emmet watched as she opened the door and disappeared. When he saw her wave to him through the window of the formal dining room, he strapped on his helmet and revved his engine. Kicking up some gravel on the driveway, he rode away.

Mara watched Emmet leave and tried to prevent her stupidly silly grin that stretched across her face when he revved the engine. Feeling like one of those sappy teenage shows where the girl was dating a forbidden man and he had just dropped her off at her dad's after keeping her out too late, she covered her face with her hands. Lowering her palms, she stared at the back of her hand where Emmet had kissed her. Raising her knuckles to her lips, she brushed the same spot and whispered, "goodnight, Emmet."

"Mara?" she heard Tom's voice and walked into the main living area of the house. "You're home."

"Yeah, sorry it's so late," she answered. "I talked to Chloe earlier. How is she?"

"She was worried about you," he said. His voice was staid. He looked like her father, sitting up waiting for her to return. A book rested on the end table along with a glass of whiskey. "Is *he* not coming in?"

"Emmet," she stressed the name knowing Tom wouldn't say it. "Thought it better if he didn't."

"Playing the victim, again," he muttered.

"I don't want to fight with you," she said. "But you're

going to have to get used to this. To us. Emmet and I are going to be seeing each other again."

"Are you now?" he asked calmly but his eyes conveyed his distain. "And I'm guessing he didn't tell you about his past?"

"Whatever is in his past is just that. In his past. You really don't know him anymore, so you have no basis for your judgement."

"Except seeing what he did to Chloe and how he almost ruined her life, but yes of course I know nothing when it comes to my former best friend."

"What could possibly cause you to hate him so much? You got the girl, you have the family. He's struggling with his past, but you are the first one to throw his sins into his face. Don't forget you're not so pearly white."

"Unlike him, I admit when I'm not pearly white."

"Unlike him? Do you even know the man anymore?"

"I know enough," he stood and downed his whiskey. "I'm trying to protect you, Mara. That man is not welcome in my house."

"No, you're not," she replied. "You're trying to protect yourself. You think Chloe's still in love with him and it eats at you. Can't you just be happy I've found someone? And you have Chloe. He cares about me, he's there for me. He doesn't want Chloe for god's sake."

"You don't know what you're talking about. You were a child," he moved to the kitchen to place his dirty glass into the sink.

"You're right I *was*. I'm not now."

"Could've fooled me. He's no good."

"He is the best man I know."

"Are you sleeping with him?" he demanded looking up at her across the sink.

"That's none of your business. I'm not a kid and you're not my father," she answered.

"Wrong, it is my business," he countered. "If you have some crazy man after you then your whereabouts are my business. I will not have this maniac come after my children looking for you. Emmet is not welcome in my house," his face contorted when he realized he said the name.

"Are you really so childish? What is your problem with him? He's a good man."

"Wrong, he is not even close to being a good man. Has he gotten you hooked on drugs yet?"

"What?" Mara took a step back.

"We are talking about Emmet O'Quinn, the drug addict, rehab failure, the cheater? Or are you talking about a different Emmet O'Quinn. Please tell me of your vast knowledge. He must be a damn good liar."

Mara was gobsmacked. She stared at Tom's face. "What?" she barely got out.

"Why do you think he broke Chloe's heart? He was in and out of rehab for two years. His last time in, he got her hooked on sleeping pills and when he dropped out again, he told her he cheated on her with one of the other patients. She was going through withdraw and he told her then. Do you know how difficult it was for her?"

"Yes," Mara replied in a small voice. "I remember."

"Don't tell me I don't know my former best friend. I lived it. He's *not* the man you think."

Tom walked around her and headed towards the stairs. "Stay away from him or you'll be hurt beyond repair. Trust me. I don't want to see you like that. Oh and another thing, my wife loves me, so I would appreciate you never saying something like that again."

With those words, he walked up the stairs and

disappeared into the darkness.

Emmet locked up his bike and headed into his flat. The moon shone brightly on the waters of the lake and he took a moment to enjoy the sight. It had been a beautiful day all around and as he walked up the flight of stairs to his loft flat, he pulled out his phone. Thinking about texting Mara and telling her how much he enjoyed the day, he unlocked his door.

He wanted to text her, but didn't quite know what to say. Did they have an actual date? Did she consider it a date? His head hurt thinking about too many possibilities. Removing his jacket, he dialed a number without thinking of the time.

"Hey, Em," Sean's sleepy voice came over the phone. "Everything all right?"

Emmet's eyes flew to the clock on his mantle. "Ah, hell Sean, I'm sorry. I didn't realize how late it was."

"No worries," Sean answered, his voice stronger but still whispered. "What's going on?"

"Ehm," Emmet grimaced. "Nothing, I'll call you back in the morning."

Emmet heard Ness's voice near the phone. "Baby, you need your rest," Sean said. Emmet couldn't hear her answer, but the phone shuffled and he heard his sister-in-law.

"Emmet?" she asked.

"Hey *cailin*," he said. "I'm sorry, love, I didn't mean to wake you. It's not all that important either."

"What is it, Em? You're always important."

Emmet smiled slightly and put her on speaker as he walked to his room, pulling off his t-shirt, riding boots and jeans. He told her about the day and how Mara had turned him inside out and upside down. When he finished, he flopped down on his bed in nothing more than his underwear and brought the phone back to his ear.

"Em, what about Trevor?" her soft question cut him deeply.

"I know," he finally sighed. "I don't know what to do."

"I just don't want you to get hurt."

Emmet wiped a hand down his face. "I know."

"Enough with that, I'm the cool sister-in-law."

"Aye, you are, lass," Emmet smiled fondly.

"So, I'm guessing you wanted to pick my brain because you want to know if she considered it a date and how to text her?" Ness asked.

"It's scary how well you know me," he chuckled.

"Yes, it is," she teased.

"So... did she? Did she consider it a date?"

"Honestly I don't know. How did you leave it? Did you both say you wanted to see each other again?"

His mind raced to their last conversation outside Tom's and Chloe's house. "Yes, she asked when she'll see me again."

"Good," she said. "Then yes, I would think she would consider it a date."

"I just can't believe how amazing she is. She didn't even flinch when I told her about Trevor."

"You told her?" she gasped.

"Well, yeah, she needed to know why I didn't kiss her."

"But you did," she pressed.

"Yeah," he sighed. She laughed at his love-sick expression.

"So, I'm guessing you want to see her again?"

"A lot, but I am worried. I don't want to hurt my chances

with Trevor's hearing."

"I know," she answered. "Listen, if you want to double date, we would be happy to join you. Or maybe you can come over for dinner and we can pretend to meet her and then conveniently head out, leaving you two alone. I know you're worried if the grandparents are having you followed."

"It's a big concern."

"You'll figure it out, I know you will. You always have great judgement."

"My judgement is a little skewed when it comes to her."

"Text her, something simple and to the point, then see what happens," Ness said. "And tell me what happens, you know how much I love family drama."

Emmet laughed. "You just want to have something new to tell the ladies next time you go to tea, so you do."

"Your mother always has the best gossip, I want to share some too!" Ness justified.

"I'll call you tomorrow, but now you need to rest."

"I already have a husband, I don't need you to tell me what to do too," she grumbled.

"Pregnancy hormones will kill my brother, I bet," he teased.

"You don't tease a pregnant lady, Em."

"I'm sure I can make it up to you. Bring you some pickles and ice cream or something."

"Ooh, now I want pickles," she replied. "Ugh… Seany…"

"I'm hanging up before I hear something I don't want to hear," he said. "Good night, Ness."

He hung up after he heard Sean demand a kiss before he would get her the bowl of pickles.

Chapter Fourteen

Emmet woke the next morning to his alarm ringing eight-thirty. His meeting with his solicitor was at ten. Reaching over for his phone to mute the alarm, his eyes rested on his text to Mara.

The read receipt showed she read the text at two-thirty that morning but hadn't texted him back. Not thinking anything of it, since they had a long night, he got up and headed to the bathroom to start his daily routine.

Still nothing as he arrived at his solicitor's office. He parked and took his phone from the dash holder. Early to the appointment, he stayed in the car and sighed. Ness's face appeared on the screen and his *Born in the USA* ringtone blared.

"Hiya," he answered.

"Hey Romeo, how did she respond?"

"She didn't," he replied. She was quiet for a beat and he let out the breath he was unconsciously holding. "That's not good. I know. What did I do wrong?"

"Hey now, it may not even have been you," she soothed. "And I've never seen you second guess yourself with a woman."

"No other woman is her," he mumbled.

"Whoa," she stated. "Who are you and what have you done with my Emmet? Playboy extraordinaire, love 'em and leave 'em?"

"It's still me, Ness, I just..." he huffed a sigh. "You're right. I'm acting like a teenager. I'm sorry. What should I care if she doesn't respond? I have ten other phone numbers of women who would jump at the chance to be with me, like."

"Mmhmm, you sound like you're trying to convince yourself."

"I hate your perceptiveness sometimes," he grumbled.

"I know," she replied. "How did you leave it with her last night?"

"I thought well, but I don't know."

"Would it hurt if you don't text her for a day? See who caves first."

"Why do women play this game?"

"And men don't?" she asked.

"Not really," he replied. Then, glancing at the clock on the dash, he sighed. "I gotta go, love, I have an appointment with my solicitor."

"It'll be okay. Don't text her. You've done your part. The ball is in her court."

"Okay okay."

"Love you, Em," she replied. "And she would be a fool to let a good man like you go."

As soon as she hung up, he shook his head. "I'm not a good man, Ness," he spoke to no one. "There are things in my past. Especially with Chloe..." he sighed again and got out of his car.

As he walked into the office building, his phone chirped. Looking down to turn it off, a text message shown and his whole body stopped.

Mara: Emmet, Tom told me some things last night. We need to talk. Please meet me. Where would be okay for you?

"Shite," Emmet cursed. Opening his phone text app, he sent a quick message back.

Emmet: Let me save some time. What he said is true, but I would like to explain.

Mara: All of it?

Swallowing hard and knowing he was about to lose her, his fingers trembled as he typed.

Emmet: Tom wouldn't lie. I'm sorry. Please meet me at Donna's Coffee Shoppe? 11:00?

When he saw she read the text but didn't reply, he closed his eyes and walked into his solicitor's office.

Emmet slowly took a sip of his coffee as he sat by the big picture window at Donna's Coffee Shoppe on the square. Well passed time to be at work for some, the coffee shop was a ghost town with only two other guests seated.

After his meeting with the solicitor, Emmet checked his phone. Mara still had yet to reply to him and as a quarter-after ticked by on the town clock, Emmet finished his coffee.

"A scone for the road, Em?" Donna asked. "You look like you could use one."

"So long as you don't tell me ma, Donna," he winked with more enthusiasm than he felt.

"Tiss, my sister got her recipe from me, you know," she replied. "Isn't it your day off today?"

"My weekend," he explained. "Thursday, Friday, then I

work until two on Saturday."

"Sunday everything is closed of course for Mass," she said. Emmet nodded. "Will you be there this Sunday?" She asked gently.

"Probably not," he answered.

"I'll say a prayer for you," she offered and headed back to get a fresh blueberry scone.

"Don't waste your breath," Emmet mumbled. He had lost his faith when his mother died after he prayed every day for healing and a cure to her incurable disease and he never got it back in all the years after.

The main door opened, and the chimes jingled. Emmet looked up and locked eyes with Tom. They said and did nothing for about thirty seconds. Emmet slowly leaned back in his chair and placed his hands on the table, one in a loose fist, ready for a fight.

"You're the last person I wanted to see," Emmet said when Tom took a seat opposite him.

"Tell me about it," Tom replied. Donna walked out with the fresh scone, stopped when she saw Tom then plastered a smile on her face. His step-mother's sister didn't know the entire history between them, all she knew was Tom had started the fight that landed them both in the hospital over ten years ago and they hadn't spoken since.

"Thomas," she greeted him. "It's nice to see you. What can I get you?"

"Coffee black, please," he replied.

"Coming up," she answered. With one final look at Emmet, she left to get Tom's coffee.

Emmet pushed the scone away from him, suddenly not hungry as he stared at his former best friend. The years had been kind to him. His massive amount of brown hair was still wavy, but Emmet did notice the few grays littering the brown depths. His eyes had faint lines around the corners as Emmet's did, a side effect of laughing and smiling too much. The face that stared back at him held so many memories, so many shenanigans and so many heartbreaks.

"How's Chloe?" Emmet asked.

"Fine," he answered.

"And the kids?"

"Fine."

"So, everyone's fine?"

"Everyone's fine," he confirmed, leaning back when Donna placed a cup of coffee in front of him.

They were quiet for a moment until Emmet finally had enough. "Why are you here?"

"I don't know," Tom sighed.

"What?"

"I saw your text on Mara's phone and decided to come here myself."

"Where's Mara?" Emmet demanded.

"Home," he replied.

"Did she not want to come?" he understood if she didn't but the way it sounded, Tom didn't tell her.

"She doesn't know," he answered. "I deleted the text before she could see it."

Emmet's fist came down on the table rattling the cups. "Dammit, Tom," he hissed. "You should have let her make up her own mind. She's an adult."

"I'm not going to let you hurt her."

"But you'll tell her things about me without allowing me to defend myself? Even for you, that's below the belt."

"Even for me? You're the one who got into that shite not

me. I didn't give you the pills."

"No, but you were always there for Chloe, weren't you," Emmet sneered.

"You broke her heart!" Tom snarled.

"And you think you can mend it?" Emmet demanded.

"I've done a damn good job over the years with her and my kids."

They were silent for a moment. "What are we doing, mate?" Emmet sighed and leaned back. "Fighting over a woman? Again? Didn't we learn anything from our broken bones the last time?"

Tom shifted uncomfortably and his hand went to his side where Emmet remembered throwing punches and hearing one of his ribs crack.

"I don't want to see Mara hurt," Tom replied.

"Neither do I."

"It was wrong of me to take her choice away from her and telling her things about you. I know you've changed but..."

"Old sins and all that," Emmet supplied.

Tom sighed. "Not only that... I still wonder if I'm enough for her."

"What?" Emmet breathed.

"There are times Chloe looks at me and it's like she's looking right through me... to you."

"What are you talking about? You're her husband. And I'm under no delusion that all of those kids are yours."

Tom nodded thoughtfully. "She conceived the first night we were together. I was an idiot and didn't wear a condom."

"The night we broke up?" Emmet clarified.

Tom nodded and looked away. "It just happened."

That stung more than Emmet was willing to admit. "I thought your eldest was eight."

"He is," Tom replied.

"The math doesn't add up."

Tom sighed and leaned back. "We lost our first. Chloe was four months and miscarried."

"Oh, man I'm sorry. I didn't know," Emmet sighed.

Tom nodded. "It was a rocky time for us, but we actually grew closer and our marriage is tighter."

"I'm glad," Emmet said. "And you don't have to worry, I'm not interested in your wife, nor is she interested in me."

"But you are interested in Mara?" Tom asked.

"I..." Emmet looked around them to make sure no one was around.

His solicitor had repeated his warning earlier that day to be extra cautious. He had received word, Trevor's grandparents had hired a private investigator to follow Emmet. When no one was around, Emmet nodded. "I am, but I can't see anyone at the moment."

"Why?"

"I have my reasons," they may be having a civil conversation for the first time in over a decade, but he wasn't going to tell him about Trevor. "What did you tell Mara?"

Tom had the decency to look ashamed. "Everything."

"Dammit, Tom," Emmet breathed.

"I'll make it right," he said.

"No," Emmet answered. "Maybe it's better this way. When everything is over, she knows what I'm talking about, then I'll contact her and see if she wants to see me. Probably won't, knowing everything."

"I'm sorry. All I saw when I looked at her was a young

Chloe. But it wasn't my place," Tom said.

"No, you're right, it wasn't, but it happened and now we've moved on."

"I'm... sorry, Emmet," Tom said. "For our fight, for Chloe, for telling Mara... everything."

Emmet leaned forward. "I'm sorry too, Tom. For the drugs, for you having to put up with my mood swings. For putting you in an awkward situation by pushing Chloe away. For our fight. For what I did to Chloe. I'm sorry."

Tom nodded and they were quiet for a moment. "I've missed this," he finally said. "I've missed our friendship."

"Me too, T," Emmet replied.

"Do you forgive me for taking Chloe away from you?"

"She was free to choose who she wanted. I'm glad I lost her to you. At least I know she's loved and well cared for."

"I do love her," he stated. "More than anything."

"I'm glad, because I would have to kick your arse from here to Dublin if you didn't," Emmet teased.

"She's a good woman," he replied.

"They both are and deserve far better than us," Emmet said.

"On that we agree," Tom replied. Looking down into his half full coffee cup, he took a deep breath. "I want you to know, I don't want anyone to get hurt again."

"I do not want to hurt anyone, let alone someone I care about. Tom, I know I have a speckled past. I have no intention of deluding her. But I wish you had let me handle it."

"She's running from something too. It scares the hell out of me."

"I know Mara would never want to put Chloe or the kids in danger."

Tom nodded as he took a swallow of his coffee. "I know she loves them and would never consciously put them in danger, but I can't be everywhere all the time. Chloe's six months. It's a scary time. She could easily lose the baby if she has a scare and she could..."

"She's strong, T, she'll be fine," Emmet said.

They were quiet again, Tom finally drained his coffee and stood. "I need to get going," he said. "I'm glad we could talk."

Emmet stood and extended his hand. "Me too."

"I'm still going to talk to Mara. She likes you and I should never have gotten in the way."

"I appreciate it, but I can't be seen with anyone right now. Mara knows this."

"Still," Tom replied. "She deserves to know what really happened. And you deserve to defend yourself."

"I'll be at my brother's later today helping paint the nursery... If she wants to call or text me."

"Cabhan or Sean?"

"Sean," Emmet confirmed.

"He bought old Larkin's place on High Street, aye?"

"Aye, he did."

"I'll tell her," Tom promised. "Do you think... nah never mind."

"I'd like to get a pint sometime, too," Emmet supplied.

"You always could read my mind," Tom said.

"Glad to know I haven't lost my touch."

"Kerry's playing Donegal next Friday."

"Old Fisherman?" Emmet asked offering the pub they used to frequent.

"Done," they shook hands and Tom left. Emmet sat back

down in his chair and stared, unseeing at the opposite seat. He and Tom had been best friends since Primary School. It was nice to be able to share a coffee without trying to rip each other's heads off.

Donna came back to clear Tom's place and put her hand on Emmet's shoulder.

"You okay?" she asked.

Being his step-mother's younger sister, Donna was only four years older than him, but she treated him like a nephew.

"Yes *auntie*, I am fine," he said.

"Tiss," she replied, giving his shoulder a smart tap. "No need to be rude." She winked. "I thought you guys weren't talking."

"We weren't," he answered. "It's amazing what women can do, eh?"

"Oh, so this is about a woman?"

"You know you're the only one in my life," he teased.

"You truly are your father's son, you flirt." Winking, he took the scone, now cold and scrunched his nose. "*Gie* it here," she ordered and took the scone back to warm it up.

CHAPTER
FIFTEEN

"Are you hungry, Emmet?" Ness's sweet voice drifted down the hall.

"Woman, I'm always hungry," he called after her fleeting figure.

Parked next to his brother's Land Rover and his father's truck, he expected more of the family to appear at any moment. The sound of his father's barrel laugh drifted down the hallway, followed by his step-mother's reproach. *Not much had changed,* Emmet thought with a chuckle.

"There he is!" his father called as he walked in to the refurbished kitchen to see his father and older brother Cabhan seated at the kitchen table. Jacks barked and raced to him. Emmet bent down to love on his pup.

"Hiya," he greeted when his dog finally allowed him to stand. His father stood and embraced him. The women; his stepmother, sisters-in-law and Ness's mother, were working around the kitchen.

"Where's Sean?" he asked when his step mom forced Ness to sit and stop working.

"Picking up supplies with Innis," Ness said.

"How's *that* possible?" Emmet asked.

"With the help of some parental intervention," his father, Orin said.

"And I refused to cook for them until they made up," his step mother, Dierdre stated as she checked something in the oven.

"Never come between an Irishman and his stomach," Cabhan's wife, Rachael said.

"Trish and I also refused... other things," Ness's face turned bright red.

Rachel laughed. "Never stand between an Irishman and *that* either."

"It worked too," Ness's and Trish's mother, Brenda replied.

"They made up and even though Sean is a little leery of trusting him, he's told me it's nice to have his brother back," Ness agreed.

"Grand, I'm happy for them. Where is Trish?" Emmet asked, sitting down in the fourth chair at the table.

"Still in Dublin, Little Cait is sick," Brenda said.

"Is she all right?" Emmet asked concerned for the newest member of their family.

"A slight fever. Innis was driving Trish crazy with checking her every two minutes, so she kicked him out to come here," Ness explained.

Emmet chuckled. Having seen his brother with his newborn baby girl, he could easily see it. She had him wrapped around her little finger.

"Anything new with the stock market?" his father asked

him as Rachael placed a beer in front of Emmet.

"Cheers, Rae," he said then turned to his father. "Things are a little dicey with the American Presidential Election looming ahead of us. My plans though are to wait it out."

"I've heard it's pretty crazy back home," Ness stated.

"A lot of conflicting views about what will happen if either of them gets into office," Emmet agreed. "I know I'm going to receive flack for this, but as a businessman myself, I can't help but wonder if he will fulfill his promises and if he does... I just might emigrate."

"Don't even talk about that," his step-mother replied smacking his arm with a wooden spoon. "You cannot leave us. I won't allow it."

"Love you too," he chuckled, rubbing his sore arm.

"Well, we'll soon find out," his father replied. "I was thinking about investing meself."

"I could give you my broker's number," Emmet offered. "He's based out of New York, but he's always available. Great guy."

"Cheers, yeah, thanks," his father said.

"You don't need another mistress, Orin," his wife stated. "First it was that bloody boat now the stock market? When do I get my husband?"

"You had me last night, love," he winked. The rest laughed and groaned at the same time.

"Hello?" Sean's voice came from the front door. "Ness, love?"

"In the kitchen," she called back. Sean and Innis came into the room, their arms laden with paint and supplies.

"Hiya, Em," Sean greeted him.

"Emmet," Innis smiled mischievously. "Just the man, there's more stuff in the car."

"You're just as capable," Emmet answered.

"Aye well, my woman has me on a strict no heavy lifting," he winked. "Says it'll decrease my sperm count."

"Can we not talk about your reproductive organs in front of the ladies?" Deirdre scolded.

"Sorry ma," he winked. "That's what happens when you're trying for another child. But Da' asked for all of it."

"Come on, lad," Orin stood and took a swig of his beer. "Let's get the lumber."

"Lumber?" Emmet questioned then groaned. "Fine," he stood beside his father, the only one of his brothers to inherit Orin's height and built.

"Here," Innis offered with a sly smile. "I even got you some gloves, so you won't get splinters."

"Piss off," Emmet snatched the gloves and followed his father down the hall.

Orin had a scare three months ago with his heart and Emmet wasn't about to lose his father especially when he needed him the most. Emmet hauled the two-by-fours around the house to the back. Once all the wood was set to the side of the platform Orin was building as an extra storage shed, Emmet sat beside him and watched as he tinkered with the drill.

"All right, spill it," Orin said without looking at him.

"Nothing to spill," Emmet sat on the platform and wiped his handkerchief across his sweaty brow.

"Lad, I've been able to read you like a book since you were born. And I've been able to tell it's a woman since you hit puberty. I'm here. And I'm a damn good listener, if you want."

Emmet took a moment to memorize his father's face. Every line, every misplaced hair, every dip and plane. The longer he stared, the stronger he realized the image mirrored his own. A longing he only recently discovered, hit him squarely in his heart. He wanted his son to look at him the same way when he was that age. And in that moment, he knew what he wanted and what to tell his father.

"He's mine, da'," he whispered the final secret he had kept from his family. Orin stopped and looked up.

"You got the paternity test back?" Orin questioned. Emmet nodded.

"I've had it for a while now," he admitted.

"I can understand why you kept it to yourself," Orin slid closer to him and placed a hand on his shoulder. "How do you feel?"

"Scared, worried I won't win. I'll never see him again. Hopeful for the future and yet ashamed at how he was conceived. I never thought twice about his mother when she left back to America after her holiday was up."

"Correct me if I'm wrong, but that is what a *holiday hook up* is, aye?" Emmet nodded and looked away. "You have nothing to blame yourself for, Em. She wanted the same." Orin waited until Emmet looked at him again. "It is the scariest thing, to become a father," Orin said. "But it is also the most incredible thing. To hold your son in your arms, to see his absolute trust and love in you..." Orin broke off for a moment and cupped his son's face. "To see the man he has become, a man who loves his family, a man who puts others before himself, there is no greater pride. You and your brothers and sister are my pride and joy. Forgive me, but I sense there is something else. You don't need to tell me, but I am here if you need to talk."

Emmet sighed. "I'm torn."

"Okay, why?"

"I want to be that little boy's father more than anything, but... you're going to think badly of me."

"Don't go borrowing trouble, lad," his father said. "I am

listening, not condemning."

After a beat, Emmet told his father everything that happened with Mara. Orin listened without reaction until he was finished.

"But it doesn't matter anymore," Emmet huffed. "She doesn't want to see me. Tom told her everything."

Orin shook his head and looked away. "I never could understand that boy. But what do you want to do, Emmet? You've already said how much you want to be Trevor's father and you just admitted you're nearly halfway in love with this girl. What does Emmet want?"

Emmet shook his head. "That's just it, da', I don't know."

"I'm not going to tell you want to do, lad," he said. "I think you need to consider what you want more than the other. Only then will you have a true path to follow."

"What if I want both?" Emmet asked.

"That's up to you. Is that an option?" Orin stated but raised his hand, stopping Emmet from speaking. "That wasn't a question I need answered. But now, how about you help me a little? Nothing settles the mind's fight quite like hard labor."

"What's your excuse then, working on that boat for the past fifteen years?" Emmet chuckled.

"I need a good workout, your mother's food was making me fat," he patted his slightly rounded belly. Emmet laughed. "I love you, son. I'm always here for you. I know some things you need to figure out on your own, but I'm here for the other stuff," he winked and pulled Emmet into a hug. "Now come on, I promised Sean I'd have this fixed up before May Day."

CHAPTER

SIXTEEN

Mara's hand shook slightly as she raised her fist to knock on the door. After a few moments of sheer silence on the other side, she checked her phone again to make sure for the tenth time she had the right address. Then she heard movement on the other side of the doorway and the door opened to reveal a young woman, heavily pregnant, dressed in leggings and an oversized cardigan sweater, her head turned back as she shouted down the hall,

"Delivery's here! Oh," she exclaimed when she turned back. "So sorry, I thought you were the furniture we ordered. Can I help you?"

"I'm sorry, I was looking for Emmet O'Quinn? I was told he would be here," Mara said.

The woman eyed her for a moment, "you must be Mara," her distinctively American accent butchered her name, but Mara smiled slightly.

"And you must be Ness? The American?" she asked.

Ness gasped playfully and slapped her hand over her heart. "What gave me away?" she teased.

"Emmet's told me a lot about you."

"Well, I am his favorite sister-in-law, but shh, don't tell the others that," she winked. "Come in. Emmet's out back helping to build my husband a new mistress."

"Ehm... what?" Mara asked as she followed Ness down the hall.

"Oh, sorry, it's a family joke," Ness threw over her shoulder. "My father-in-law spends so much time out in his shed, my mother-in-law has dubbed it his mistress."

"Oh," Mara replied. "I see." Suddenly, she felt an overwhelming sense of unease. Emmet was with his family and all day she thought he had ignored her text. At least, until Tom had called to tell her what he had done. It didn't take much for him to urge her to go see Emmet and, had her brother-in-law been there, she would have chewed him out good and proper, but he wasn't and she couldn't scream at him over the phone. So she got dressed and headed to the address Tom had sent her. Still leery of what Tom had told her the night before, Mara wasn't about to judge someone by their past, but she needed the whole truth.

"Can I ask you something?" Ness had stopped in the middle of the hallway and turned to her. Mara nodded. "Why didn't you answer his text last night?"

Her face gave nothing away but if Ness had super human hearing, she would hear her heart beating far too fast.

"I – ehm," she started. "Needed some time to clear my head. It all happened so quickly and with our history... I just needed some time."

Ness was silent for a moment, absently stroking her protruding stomach. "I understand," she said. "When I first met my husband, things were difficult and we both needed time, but may I say something?" At her nod, Ness continued. "Emmet is the best man I know, apart from my husband. He helped me through some difficult times over a year ago. He has a speckled past, I know, but he is worth every bit of your time. Trust me." Mara was silent for a moment but finally nodded. "With that said," Ness perked up. "You hurt him, I'll kill you." She grinned and Mara blinked, unsure if she was serious or not. "Come on, I'll introduce you."

"Ness, love?" a man's voice made them turn. He and another man stood on the stairs, paint splatter on their faces and hands. "Our furniture's here?"

"Sorry, babe," she answered. "False alarm. This is Mara, she's here to see Emmet."

"Oh aye?" the other man asked with a strange grin. "And why?"

"That's none of our business, Innis," Ness replied sweetly.

"Have you warned her about ma? She'll be worse than me," the man's grin grew.

"I was just about to. Don't you have some more to paint?"

"Ooh, harsh," Innis answered.

"Come on, Inn," Sean stated slapping his brother's back. "Let's finish up. I want to be with my wife, and I can smell Ma's cooking from here."

Sean and Innis headed up the stairs with a wink to Ness. "Sorry, that's my husband and his brother. They're painting the baby's room."

"They look like Emmet," Mara nodded.

Ness tilted her head, regarding her. "Somewhat," she answered. "They are brothers."

"Right, of course," Mara stopped herself and nodded.

"Come on," Ness smiled and waddled down the hall toward the voices in the kitchen and Mara took a moment to collect herself before following.

The kitchen was busy with three women cooking and Ness standing near the entrance.

"Everyone, this is Mara," she announced as Mara turned a corner to see them.

"Hiya, Mara," the women said at once but then returned to their duties.

"She's here to see Emmet," Ness's tone was almost conspiratorial.

One of the older women stopped and turned to look at her. "And what would ye be wanting with my Emmet?"

"I just need to talk to him," Mara answered.

"Oh aye? What about?" the woman asked.

"Dierdre," the other older woman spoke. "Leave the poor girl alone. You really can be intimidating."

"Aye, that's what I like about me," she replied. "But this woman wants to speak to my Emmet and she better no' be here causing him pain or trouble."

"Deirdre is Emmet's and my husband's step-mother," Ness whispered to Mara.

"Leave the lad be, he's thirty-six," the older woman said.

"And that's my mom," Ness spoke again. "They've been best friends since before I was born. Her husband, my uncle is away on business until the end of the week."

"That depends," Deirdre stated. "On her motive to see my lad."

"I'm sorry, Mom, but I agree with Mama. Emmet's business is his own," Ness said, then looked slyly at Mara. "You'll find him out back," Ness hooked her thumb over her right shoulder indicating the back door. Mara thanked her and excused herself from the room.

"She better not be causing any trouble for my lad, that's all I have to say," she heard Deirdre's comment follow her out.

Emmet hadn't said much about his stepmother on their day trip except that he owed her a lot and she treated the four brothers like her own. Had Mara not been so nervous, she admitted, she would have enjoyed bantering back and forth.

Slipping out the back door onto a deck, she raised her hand over her brow to shade her eyes from the early afternoon sun.

"Hiya," she jumped when she heard a voice beside her. "Sorry, didn't mean to frighten you." A man in his early forties stood from the deck chair where he was staining two-by-four planks of wood. "Can I help you?"

"Sorry," Mara answered. "I'm looking for Emmet?"

"In the shed," he nodded toward a copse of trees and a two-sided building. Looking over, she saw an older man with strikingly similar features to Emmet, sanding a smaller piece of wood but didn't see the man she needed to see. "Is there something I can help with?" The man beside her asked.

"No, thank you," Mara said. "I just need to find him."

"I'm Cabhan, his older brother," he replied offering his hand.

"Mara," she stated accepting the shake.

"At least you managed to survive the women," he teased. "I'm surprised Ma didn't interrogate you on the spot."

"She did," Mara replied. "But with Ness's help I was able to escape."

"Ha, my sister-in-law is fearless, must be the American in her," he said.

"Probably," she agreed. Their conversation now stale, Mara looked back over to the shed when she heard Emmet's voice.

"Gie it a try now, da'," he called, his Irish accent stronger as he grunted under some unseen labor or pressure. "I tink I got it."

The older man stopped sanding and headed over to the far side of the shed. Hoisting the wall up from the ground using a pully, the frame of the wall began to rise until it was vertical and then the whirling of a pneumatic drill echoed across the lawn. Mara held her breath when the sound stopped and Emmet walked out and down the two steps of the shed, dusting off his jeans.

"There, got it tightened up. Figured it out. The footing was off a little," he explained.

"There's nothing wrong with my footing," the older man stated as he came around the corner laughing.

"Aye aye, well sometimes we all make mistakes," Emmet winked.

"I'll have you know, young man there is nothing wrong with my plans, everything was accurate," the older man teased.

"You ain't perfect, da'," Emmet laughed. "As ma reminds you every day."

"That's no' what she was saying last night," he ribbed. Emmet barked a laugh and reached for his beer, taking a long swig.

"Em," Cabhan called making Mara jump as she stood beside him. Emmet looked over and froze. "You have a visitor."

"Mara?" Emmet questioned.

"Mara?" the older man asked. Emmet didn't look over at his father, his eyes never left hers. "Well, what are you waiting for? Get over there."

It took him a moment, but soon Emmet was walking across the lawn to the deck. Mara's hands were sweaty and her heart raced. Emmet stood before her, four steps down, but they were eye to eye.

"What are you doing here?" he asked softly.

"Tom told me where you were and what he did," she answered.

"Tom?" Cabhan took a step forward. "What does he have to do with this?"

"Cabh," his father called as he walked up behind Emmet. "Let's go inside, lad. I can smell your mother's cooking from out here." To his credit, Cabhan did not argue and turned on his heels back to the house. "Take your time," his father whispered as he passed them.

CHAPTER
SEVENTEEN

Emmet couldn't believe Mara was there. Tom had told him he was going to tell her about deleting her text, but never in his dreams did he expect Mara to show up at his brother's house looking for him.

"I'm really glad to see you," he said.

She wrung her hands but didn't look up at him for a little while. Emmet let her think until she finally raised pleading eyes to him.

"Emmet, I'm sorry, I didn't know you asked me to meet you. I had set my phone down, open to your text when I went to help Chloe in the kitchen and Tom saw it. Before I knew what happened, he had erased it. You must think I'm a horrible person. You need to know, I am the *last* person to ever judge someone by their past. Please believe me. I am so sorry. I just needed clarification and time to process. When I reread what I sent to you, I realized how it must have been taken, but honestly, I merely needed to hear the whole story, I never meant it as a rebuke. Chloe has never said a bad thing about you and to hear that side of things was..."

"Eye opening?" he offered.

"Unnerving," she replied. "To me, growing up, you were perfect. I measured every guy I met against you." He tried to hide his smirk but could not stop himself from puffing out his chest a little. "It's true. You were the best man I knew and when things ended with you and Chloe, I didn't know what to think. I hated you for leaving her, but I also hated you for shattering my idea of a perfect man. I'm older now and I know there aren't perfect men in the world, everyone has a past. But of anyone... you're still the closest to perfect."

"I'm flattered," he said. "But don't put me on a pedestal. I don't deserve it. I'm flawed. But I would do anything to take away the hurt I caused you both," his eyes drifted over her shoulder to see the drapes in the living room move and he let out a soft chuckle. "Listen, I want to talk more about this, but my family is ridiculously curious about you and I'm afraid if we go to get a pint, they'll just follow us and feign surprise that we ran into them. Can we talk Sunday? I'll skip mass if you will," he winked.

Mara laughed. It had been years since she attended church. "Sure, want me to meet you somewhere?" At his hesitation, she continued. "I could meet you at your favorite view."

He nodded. "That'd work."

"Ten?" she asked.

"Aye," he agreed.

"Now, what can I do to help?" she asked.

"Ehm, well, if you want but we have a lot of people. My cousin Keera and sister Sinéad will be over with wine and champagne soon along with some sparkling water for Ness. We wanted to get the shed done but I don't know what the women are doing."

"I don't mind some hard work," she tentatively reached

forward and dusted off wood shavings from his grey t-shirt. "What's the story? Just so I'm prepared if they ask."

"Stick with the truth. There's no secrets between my family and me," Emmet said.

"And if they press?"

"If they do, just smile and I'll take over," he replied. Taking her lower lip between her teeth, she finally nodded. Emmet reached up and passed his thumb over her lip releasing it from between her teeth. "You know what biting your lip does to me?" she shook her head. Taking a step up to her, he lowered his voice. "It makes me jealous. I'm not a jealous man, but you keep doing that, I'll have to show you what lip biting actually is." Slowly, she sunk her teeth into her lower lip and locked eyes with him. "You play with fire."

"I'm not afraid to be burnt," she answered.

After a beat, he took a step back. "You should be."

Emmet and Mara walked into the house to see everyone immediately jump into doing something, covering the fact they had been watching. Emmet chuckled beside her and rolled his eyes.

"All right, all right, you can all stop pretending," he called out. Everyone stopped and looked at them. "I know you're all curious so, this is Mara. She's Chloe's sister and... well, we are..." he looked at her and she nodded. "Sort of, seeing each other."

Everyone stared for a moment then bursts of congratulations started. Deirdre came over and hugged her.

"I should have known," she said. "The resemblance is striking but you are much prettier than your sister."

"Thank you," she answered shyly.

"Ma, come now," Emmet said. "Don't make her uncomfortable within five seconds."

"Uncomfortable? I would never," she replied horrified. "I merely speak the truth."

"Sometimes the truth is uncomfortable, love," Orin said saddling up beside his wife. "Nice to meet you, Mara, I'm Orin."

"My da'," Emmet introduced.

"A pleasure," she replied. "I didn't mean to interrupt. I needed to speak with Emmet."

"Nonsense, girl," Orin answered. "You didn't interrupt anything."

"You are more than welcome to stay," Ness said. "My mother and mother-in-law always fix too much food. And though I'm eating for two, I can't be expected to eat it all."

"You're beautiful, love," her husband came up beside her and dropped his arm around her waist. "Sean O'Quinn," he introduced. "Good to meet you."

"Likewise," Mara replied. "Is there anything I can do to help? I'm not a gourmet chef but I know my way around the kitchen."

"Could you put the lattice on the pie?" Deirdre asked and Emmet saw the challenge in his stepmother's eyes. She was testing Mara. He sighed, supposing it should be expected.

"Absolutely," she answered. Emmet chuckled at Deirdre's surprised expression. "Just point me to the pastry and let me wash my hands."

Deirdre nodded slowly and walked with her to the sink. His father clapped a hand on his shoulder as they watched Mara wash her hands and roll up her sleeves to get to work. Catching Ness's eye, Emmet raised his eyebrows. Ness grinned and nodded, he had her blessing. And just like that, his woman was welcomed by his family. Now all he had to do was get through the hearing and somehow help Mara with that bastard ex of hers.

Chapter Eighteen

"You really didn't have to walk me the whole way," Mara said as they arrived at Tom's and Chloe's front door.

"I know," Emmet replied. "But I wanted to."

"Good," she smiled. "I had such a good time today meeting your family."

"Yeah, they're gas," Emmet stated. "I love them."

"And they love you."

Emmet nodded. "I know. I'm lucky."

Mara stepped up to the front door but turned back to him. They stared at each other for a long moment until Emmet spoke.

"Do you have any idea how much I want to kiss you right now?"

"Tell me," she said.

"I want it more than I do my next breath."

"Tell me what you would do."

"I would wind my arm around your lower back, pulling you flush against me," he described.

"And then?" her voice breathy.

"My hand would weave into your hair, and I would pull gently but with power, so you know just who has control, and then I tease your lips until you beg and whimper my name."

"I'm not much of a whimperer," she replied.

"You will be," he whispered. They locked eyes for a long while and she noticed the subtle changes in his face as he debated kissing her. Just as he leaned forward, the front door opened, and she gave a little yelp as she danced away from Emmet. Tom stood in the doorway and looked between them.

"Emmet," Tom said.

"Tom," Emmet replied.

"Thank you for walking her home," Tom answered.

"My pleasure," Emmet said. "Thank you for explaining things."

Tom nodded but said nothing more. After a moment, he looked over at Mara and indicated for her to come in. "It's late."

"You're right," Mara agreed. "I'll see you later?" Mara turned to Emmet.

Emmet said nothing, not giving away their plans to meet Sunday. She stepped around Tom and into the house. Tom looked at Emmet and gave a single nod before retreating and closing the door. Emmet stood on the stoop, hoping to see a glimpse of Mara but when he realized how long he waited there, he shuffled down the drive, kicking the gravel as he went. The sound of a window opening drew his attention. Turning, he looked up to the second floor to see Mara lean out. Her smile took his breath away. Waving, she blew him a kiss, like a teenager. He pretended to catch it and blew her one back. Looking over her shoulder, she glanced back at him and pulled in, lowering the window.

Sunday morning, Emmet woke to the sun shining across his face. Jacks lay beside him, his old eyes watching him. Stroking the lab's soft head, he smiled.

"Hey lad," he said softly. "Watching me again?" Jacks moved his brows as if debating but got up slowly and licked his face.

Jacks had been a rescue when he was only one year old. He was a gift to an elderly father who had just lost his wife, but the older man couldn't look after the lab and one day Jacks woke to his owner having passed away in the middle of the night. His barking drew people's attention as they walked by but, being so remote it had been two days. Jacks was so scared the first time Emmet went with his brother Cabhan, a veterinarian, to meet him at his surgery. The poor pup had shied away from him, his tail tucked between his legs. Immediately, Emmet knew he wanted him. If he could have a dog as screwed up as he was maybe it would help him. It took Emmet over six months to have his dog trust him enough to sleep beside him. He owed that crazy lab so much over the years. Not wanting bad memories to ruin the day, he stroked his dog's boney head and sat up.

"Let's get you something to eat, eh?" he asked framing the old grey and black face in his hands. Swinging his legs over the edge of the bed as his dog slowly found a way down, he rubbed a spot on his chest that ached as he saw the old dog's shuffled gait and slow movements. He couldn't bear to lose him.

Grabbing his sweatpants and white t-shirt, he pulled them on and headed to the kitchen. It was only eight-thirty, he had plenty of time to feed Jacks, make himself a bagel sandwich and warm up one of Deirdre's scones before he jumped in the shower to be ready to meet Mara at his favorite view by ten. As he sat at his kitchen table and chewed his first bite of a sausage, egg and cheese bagel, he watched absently as his dog ravenously attacked the food in his bowl.

The church bells tolled the hour and the call to Mass. He hadn't been to Mass in years, but he always felt a little guilty knowing his parents would be looking for him until it almost made them late. Once the tolling stopped and he finished his sandwich, scone and orange juice, he stood from the table, put his dishes in the sink and headed to the shower. The hot water felt good on his aching shoulders. A regular gym goer, he was still unaccustomed to manual labor and carrying thirty two-by-fours from his brother's truck to the backyard and then helping his father hoist up the three walls of the shed had tightened muscles he didn't know existed.

Jacks lounged in a sliver of sunlight and raised his brows when Emmet left his room, dressed in jeans, a grey t-shirt and a black button up Aran sweater, unbuttoned. Grabbing Jacks' lead, he looked over at his black lab. His tail started to wag slowly. He remembered when Jacks would jump up and race circles around his ankles when he saw the lead. Knowing his dog was getting old, worried him.

Kneeling down, he took Jacks' old white face in his hands and cradled his head. "Walkies, lad?" he asked. Jacks' tongue flicked out and licked his chin. Smiling, he ruffled the dog's fur and attached the lead. Heading down the inside stairs of the complex, he saw Mara's small red car in the parking lot. She was early.

The sun hit him directly in the eyes, but he heard the door open and close then Mara was there. Without thinking, he grabbed her to him and kissed her, hard.

"Well well, good morning," she teased when she could speak.

"Good morning, beautiful," he answered. "I hope you don't mind, but Jacks needed a walk and well, you both mean a lot to me, so I wanted you to meet properly."

She looked down at the dog, gazing up at his master and smiled. Crouching down, she clenched her hand into a soft fist and held it out to his dog to sniff.

"Hiya, Jacks," she said. "It's good to meet you." The dog whimpered and licked her hand. She grinned and stroked the boney head.

Looking up at Emmet, her smile was brilliant and his chest ached. Even though it was silly, she passed his dogs approval.

"Ready?" He asked once she was upright.

"Ready," she answered. They turned together and began to walk along the bank of the loch.

"Thank you for meeting me," Emmet started.

"Thank you for letting me. I'm still angry with Tom for what he did."

"He thought he was protecting you."

"Reading and deleting my texts without my knowing?"

"Aye, I know his methods were wrong, but he meant well and it gave us a chance to speak. We are getting a pint Friday."

She stopped. "Really?"

"You're surprised. So am I," he admitted. "But it's kind of nice."

She was quiet for a long moment before she stopped and turned to him. "Emmet, I need to know everything. I know what Tom said, but I need to hear it from you."

Emmet took a deep breath but nodded.

"Aye, well," swallowing, he continued. "Tom wouldn't lie but I am glad you let me tell my side. Chloe and I were together for five years and we were going to be married. But my mother died when I was sixteen, just a few months after I met you and your family. It was a very difficult time for me but when my dad met Deirdre a year later, I was angry he could move on so quickly. I don't know if you remember any of this, but I actually ran away from home and went to Dublin."

Mara nodded and he went on.

"When I got there, I was living on the streets and fell into the wrong crowd. I wanted something to take the pain away. The dealers I met gave me Oxycodone. Angry with the world, the drugs were a way for me to have a slight reprieve from my life. I didn't care that it was wrong, and yes, I knew it was, but I needed to get away from the pain. The way it was explained to me was, the pills would be a stress and grief relief. And they were until I couldn't get enough and was popping pills for the slightest thing. I was on the street for six months." He shook his head and sighed. Mara took his hand and held it a gentle comfort.

"My dad eventually finally found me. Never has told me how, but one day I looked up from my cot, still high and saw him standing over me. He was concerned and yet it was the disappointment in his eyes I still remember. He picked me up and carried me out to a waiting taxi. Next thing I remember was my dad sitting beside me holding my hand crying. The high was wearing off and no matter what, he wouldn't give me anything for the pain slowly creeping in. The withdrawal was the hardest part. Seeing my dad there every day, having him hold my shoulders as I wracked with heaves over the toilet. Having him apply a cool cloth when I was sweating it out. The worst and the best part was, he was always there. He's seen me at my lowest and still loved me. When the worst was over, he got me into a taxi and took me to a center, a hospital of sorts. He told me I was going to be staying there for a little while. It was my intervention. I hated him again but deep down I knew it was for the best. I was there for three years, on and off. Chloe came to see me a few times when I was allowed visitors. But I was desperate for more drugs, so I... begged her to get me some pills. She smuggled in some of your ma's antidepressants. And to my eternal shame, I forced her to try them first. Not that I held her chin open or anything, but I told her if she loved me, she would try it. It's my greatest regret apart from cheating on her with one of the other patients."

"Tom told me you did," she said softly.

"I wish I could say it wasn't true. I was released later that week and when I got home, told her about it as she was coming down off a high. I believe it is what pushed Chloe over the edge. She downed a few pills, had to have her stomach pumped. She nearly died. I'll never forgive myself for what I put her through."

"Who told you that?"

"Tom, when he sought me out at the pub later that night. We beat the shite out of each other."

"Emmet," she stopped walking. "Chloe never downed the pills. She wanted to but I came in to her room when she held them in her hand and stopped her. She cried to me all night. She was so angry at you for cheating on her, she convinced Tom to sleep with her to get back at you but then realized how much she actually cared for him. She was so confused and while she was asleep, I called Tom, telling him what she tried to do. That must have been when he told you."

Emmet was silent for a while. "He lied?" He finally asked.

"I'm sure it was only because he was angry."

Shaking his head, he tried to clear it. "I have hated myself for nearly twenty years because of what I thought I had done to her."

"Please, it wasn't anyone's fault. Everyone takes some of the blame in this."

"Apart from you," he said softly, stroking her face.

"Even me," she admitted. "I hated you and did nothing to stop them from being together."

"That's not anything to be blamed for," he replied. "You were protecting your family. And I was an arse."

She slipped her hand into his. "You were a part of that family for a time. I always loved you."

"I never realized, I always cared for you. Now, I see the woman you grew into and all I have to say is, I am damned lucky you want me."

"Yes, you are," she winked and raised to her toes to kiss him. "I will always want you and will always wait for you. I hope you still want me even when you're a father."

He breathed a laugh, "always, love. It's hard to believe, but I love that little boy."

"I would like to meet him someday."

"You will," he answered.

"When is the court date?"

"My solicitor says it could be scheduled any day now. I'll have a week's notice, though."

"Is there anything I can do? Character witness maybe?"

"Maybe," he chuckled. "But they'll be exposing my relationship with Chloe and my stint in rehab along with my philandering. I'm worried."

"That was years ago."

"It doesn't matter. It shows my character."

"You were a man whose mother just died, anyone would be sympathetic. And you are a successful businessman, now. You could provide a stable home for your son."

"I just don't want his grandparents to take him away. They live in America and I'll never see him again if they get him."

"Don't think like that," she said. "You can't afford to."

He stopped for a moment and took a deep breath. Sliding his arm around her, he pulled her close to him. Lowering his lips to hers, he glided his tongue across the seam of her lips. She opened gladly and he plunged in, tasting her. She reached up and ran her fingers through his hair, latching on, digging her nails into the amber depths. Finally, they both pulled back when Jacks whimpered beside them. Panting and flushed, they locked eyes and something inside Emmet's heart burst. He had to ask her something important.

"Would you be willing... My parents have a place up in

Sligo. It's remote. We could go there together."

"After the hearing?"

He shook his head, "I could be waiting months for you. I can't do that."

"I won't let you lose this case simply because of our lust for each other. Keep it in your pants, O'Quinn."

He chuckled and was about to pull her into him again when her phone rang. Pulling it out, a frown on her face, she looked at the number. It wasn't registered. Answering it, she put it to her ear.

"Hello?"

She waited. He couldn't hear anything on the other end and soon he understood why. "Look, Ben, I'm not in the mood. You lost. Leave me alone."

"Never," a voice stated.

"So, it is you," she gasped. Emmet pulled the phone from her hand and spoke into the receiver.

"Listen here, you little shite," he began. "You leave Mara alone. You don't own her. She is her own person. You ever call her again, you will have to deal with me. And you probably already know what I can do to pencil pushers like you. Leave my girlfriend alone."

"You'll regret this. She is mine."

"Wrong, she is no one's. She is her own person. Now leave us alone before I ask my cousin to have a talk with the *Garda Síochána na hEireann*." He hung up and handed the phone back to Mara.

"Girlfriend?" she asked. Emmet shrugged.

"What else? Unless you don't want to be."

"I do but I'm worried. He won't stop," she whispered.

"Then I look forward to the arrest. My cousin is the Deputy Mayor. You don't mess with what's mine."

"I'm not yours."

"You are, make no mistake," he drew her closer. "Come with me to my parent's cabin, girlfriend."

She stared at him for a long moment but then nodded. "Aye, Emmet. I'll come with you."

CHAPTER

NINETEEN

Friday came sooner than Emmet expected and as he walked into the Old Fisherman, a local he hadn't been to in years, he saw Tom sitting at the bar nursing a pint of Guinness. Terrance, the bartender and son of the owner, saw him, his eyes wide as his gaze fell on Tom. Terrance went to primary with them and the whole town heard when they fell out, let alone the damage the pub had sustained from their fight. Emmet smiled and slid into the seat next to Tom, slapping him on the back as he settled.

"Pint please, Terry," he ordered. Tom looked over at him for a moment then a soft smile lifted his lips.

"I almost didn't show," he admitted.

"Me neither," Emmet replied. "But then I thought, what the hell." Emmet's Guinness was placed before him and Terrance gave them both a wary stare.

"Looks like someone heard about our row," Tom took a drink.

"Aye, I think all of Ireland knows this is the first time we've been in the same pub without trying to kill each other. I'm still barred from Old McCarthy's."

"Me too. But do you honestly still think you'd beat me in a fight?"

"I know I would," Emmet chuckled.

"In your dreams, Em," Tom laughed but raised his glass to him. "To friendship, may it grow as we may wind up being brothers anyway."

Emmet nearly choked on his own saliva. "What?" He asked.

"You and Mara," Tom said. "I overheard her tell Chloe you were going to Sligo together tomorrow."

Emmet immediately looked around trying to see if anyone heard. "That's still undecided."

"I thought so," he nodded. "Considering the last time I talked to you, you said you couldn't see anyone at the moment. Care to tell me why you're hell-bent on seeing her?"

Emmet took a drink to fortify his nerves. Tom was acting like her father.

"You were my best friend and as such, I feel the need to explain but that title was long ago and though I hope we can mend at least some of the past, do not think for one second I owe you an explanation."

"Understood, but she is living with my family. If you're mixed up in whatever is haunting her, it could affect my kids."

"Whatever she is mixed up in, it has nothing to do with me."

"Then what are you mixed up in?" Tom demanded.

Emmet took a deep breath, a long draw on his beer, and decided it would be better to tell him.

"I have a kid," he stated. Tom coughed and sputtered

into his beer.

"What?" He asked. "Jaysus," wiping his mouth, he looked up at him. "Who with?"

"That's not important, but what is, is his mother died recently and I got a letter from her. She was American, and her parents are suing for custody. They're trying to paint me as a player, a philanderer, an unfit father. I never knew about him and her last request was I raise him, that is my defense. But my solicitor says it's weak and I need to stay away from women, drinking in excess, and pretty much any behavior that would sway a judge. I've been fine with that, until recently. The difficulty is, I've fallen for Mara. I don't know how to play this out. But I've met my son and I... I've fallen in love with him too. I wouldn't want to do anything that would put an end to it. But god, I love Mara. She is willing to wait, but I'm not. I don't want to. She's amazing, wonderful, beautiful, the most incredibly strong woman I've ever met. I don't know, mate. I want to be with her, and I want to be a father. I never thought I would have a child. You know that. I don't know what to do." Emmet took a long drink of his beer, waiting for Tom to speak.

Tom was quiet for a long moment, his eyes fascinated by the foam in his beer. Finally, he looked over. "I've never seen you like this before."

Emmet shrugged. "I've never been a father before."

Tom nodded, slowly. "I've been there."

They said nothing for a little while but soon Tom downed his beer, motioned for another and turned back to Emmet. "I've been your friend for decades. Yes, we've had our knock down drag out fights, and yes, I hated you for several years. But my wife and I have talked. She has and always will love me and she doesn't see you when she looks at me. Seeing you like this; willing to do anything for your child, hoping for a future with a woman who cares deeply for you and who you care deeply for in return, has completely changed my opinion of you. Chloe has already told Mara this, but I will say it to you, we will not stand in your way and if my sister-in-law and you want to pursue, this we will back you. But know this, Mara is my family I will protect her and if she decides to go with someone else... don't look to me to try to sway her. But you *are* different. You have changed. And I want to help you. What can I do? How can I help you win your dream? You deserve this. You deserve to be a father and have the love of your life, just like I have. So tell me, my friend, what can I do?"

Emmet was stunned. Just like that, he had his best friend back.

"What?" Tom asked.

Emmet realized he was staring. "Sorry, I guess I never expected to hear that from you."

"Honestly, I never expected to say it. But Em, I'm tired. I'm tired of always wondering, worrying if Chloe had a chance, would she leave me and go with you. I know now that's not true, but I wasted so long worrying. I'm tired of hating you. I'm tired of pretending. I've... been out of work for a while and I haven't told anyone. I've pretended, kept it all in and it's too much. It's just too much." He wiped his hand down his face.

"What?" Emmet questioned. "What happened? I thought you got promoted."

"I did, then there was an accusation... I spoke harshly to an employee, a female employee. I was let go."

"You haven't told anyone? Even Chloe?" Emmet asked gently.

"No, with the baby coming, she can't handle any more stress. I've been pretending. Getting up, going out, looking for work, but there's nothing. I have a little money put aside that we've been living on, but it's draining quickly. If I don't get something soon, we won't make the house payment. What will I do then?"

Emmet placed his hand on his friend's shoulder and squeezed. "What salary do you need?"

"At least forty thousand," he answered. "My parents paid

the house off, but we did an update to the kitchen and took a loan out, isn't much but with the baby and the kids... Nothing else will be enough."

"Can you start next week?"

"What?"

"Monday? I need another salesman. Base is forty-two plus commission."

Tom looked at him, an uneasy look in his eyes. "That's not why I wanted to have a beer with you."

"I know that. But honestly. I need another salesman. I know you. It's yours if you want. Monday morning ten o'clock. Please, Tom."

Tom took a breath. "Thank you," he sighed. "I need it. I would say I don't, but I can't put Chloe through it. Thank you."

"Don't thank me. Just because you have a job doesn't mean I won't expect you to work," he winked.

"I can sell, you know that," he answered.

"You'll have to prove to me you're better at sales because I know how good you are at mechanics. If I had an opening, I would get you in the shop. I know how much you love tearing down and putting back together."

"Your first car, I put together for you," he chuckled and took a long draw on his beer.

"I know it," Emmet replied motioning for another beer. "So, come on, I know we've been apart for years but you were my best friend since I was seven. I won't see you suffering when I have a chance for you. And you're married to someone who meant a lot to me. Besides it looks like we might be seeing more and more of each other if this thing with Mara works out."

"I don't know what else to say but, thank you."

"You're welcome. You'll be working mainly with Paddy and me. We have a few part time salesmen, but they are only when Paddy and I take time off. For me, like this weekend. You remember Paddy?"

"I do," he answered. "Is he still a player?"

"Of course, though I haven't seen him with anyone recently, not sure if he's found someone."

"God forbid," Tom chuckled.

"Heaven help the woman," Emmet replied.

Tom raised his glass toward Emmet. "I've missed you, my friend. To your future with your son and the woman of your dreams."

"Nothing's set yet," Emmet raised his beer.

"I know, but let's dream like we did when we were kids. Dream for two hours. And get completely bolloxed."

"Cheers to that!" Emmet laughed and clinked his glass to Tom's. Turning back to the television they watched the game and ordered some food.

Tom could not hold his liquor as well as he used to, nearly ten years ago and was barely able to stay upright after his sixth beer. Emmet, on the other hand, had a much higher tolerance and was careful not to be seen drinking too much.

When the hurling match was over, their county winning, Emmet settled the bill and got Tom up. After a quick text to Mara letting her know he'd be bringing Tom home, he helped him walk to the door.

"Where are we going?" Tom's slurred question beside Emmet's ear, surprised him.

"I'm getting you home."

Tom swung his head over to look at Emmet. "I still don't know where we stand with each other. Part of me wants to punch you and part of me wants to kiss you."

Emmet chuckled. "You have a wife; how would she look upon you kissing random men trying to get you home?"

Tom giggled and couldn't stop. "I'd think she'd have me sleep on the couch, so she would."

"Then resist my charms and good looks so you can sleep next to your wife tonight," Emmet teased.

Tom laughed. "You know that's right where I want to be."

"You are a smart man," Emmet replied.

"Are we really going to be brothers?" Tom asked. Emmet's steps faltered and Tom cried out excitedly. "Whoa! Hey!" He began singing some nonsensical song giving Emmet a chance to think about his words. It was the second time Tom had mentioned that and it made Emmet wonder. Was that what Mara was saying when home? Or was it their perception? Whatever it was, Mara and he were leaving for Sligo for a weekend together. One time or another he may need to bring it up. He was not in any position to propose, he didn't have a ring... He shook his head. Instead of saying his usual mantra when a woman got too clingy of, *I'm not ready to settle down,* or *I'm in no position to be in anything long term* his main reasoning for not marrying was because he didn't have a ring? What was wrong with him? He refused to think any more on it and focused instead on getting his drunk friend home then prepare for the weekend. He had switched his time off to be Friday through Sunday so he could spend the weekend in Sligo.

As soon as he got Tom home, he would head back to his apartment, would feed Jacks, shower and pack. Since his plan did not include many clothes, if any at all, he would pack light. While Tom continued to sing a very drunken version of *Whiskey in the Jar,* Emmet's thoughts wandered to Mara. Could he actually be considering proposing? Yes, they had only been together for a couple weeks, but they had known each other for decades. Her ex bothered him more than he cared to admit but after they had gone to the police, that first day before their motorcycle ride, he felt a little better. Until Benjamin was behind bars, Emmet would never cease watching over his shoulder. The calls and texts had stopped but that didn't mean he was going away. If Emmet had learned one thing last year with Ness's stepfather is was that they can appear when you least expect them.

Realizing with a start, he hadn't been paying attention to where they were, he was thankful Tom had moved into his parent's old house when they passed away. Emmet knew the way instinctually and as soon as the old stone cottage came into view, he breathed a sigh of relief even as knots formed in his belly at the prospect of seeing Mara. *Christ man, you have it bad,* he thought when the door opened, and Mara appeared.

"As promised," Emmet teased, indicating Tom. Chloe appeared behind her sister.

"Tom," she scolded.

"My wife!" Tom called and stumbled forward. "Dammit, you're sexy, mmm." He wrapped his arms around her and took a deep whiff of her hair. "You always smell so good."

Mara and Emmet laughed as Chloe rolled her eyes and walked Tom into the living room leaving them alone. When she locked eyes with him, her face softened.

"I'll pick you up tomorrow?" he whispered.

She nodded. "Two o'clock."

Emmet stroked her cheek. "I cannot wait."

"Me neither."

"Tomorrow then." Emmet resisted kissing her. "I'll see you then."

She stepped back inside and slowly closed the door. Emmet moved away but kept his eyes on her until the door shut firmly.

Tomorrow. Mara McGrath would be his. Tomorrow.

Chapter Twenty

Emmet opened the door of the cottage and let Mara enter first. Having been there hundreds of times before, he stood by the door and watched. She lowered the hood of her coat and looked around. The front opened to a spacious living room, partitioned from the old country kitchen by a small floor to ceiling wall with a painting of the countryside hanging at eye level. The stairwell going up to the bedrooms was to their right and the sliding door at the back wall over looked the sea and mountain range. Emmet tried to look at it as a first-time visitor and he had to say he was proud of what he saw.

When Mara turned to him, a wide smile on her face, he knew he had chosen well, not just in location but in woman. He figured she was expecting to fall into bed as soon as they got there, but Emmet wanted to take it slower for the first time in his life. He offered his hand to her; the simple gesture, one he had done a thousand times before, different meanings behind each one. With Mara, it felt different than all the others. It wasn't merely a helping hand as it was to his sister or mother, nor was it a blatant invitation to his bed as it was with so many others before her. No, with Mara it was an invitation for him. Not his body, not his help... him. All of him. He offered so much in that one outstretched hand.

Almost as if she knew the depth behind the gesture, Mara hesitated just a moment before confidently taking his hand in hers and holding it. He slowly reached forward with his other hand and lowered the zipper of her coat all the way down. She stood silently, allowing him to take control. Emmet turned her gently and pulled the coat off her shoulders and down her arms. Her hair had been pulled up into a messy pony tail and the boat neck shirt she wore exposed the expansive creamy skin of her neck and shoulders. Emmet couldn't help himself and lowered his lips to her skin, placing gentle whisper kisses, each one softer than the last. Mara's increased breathing sent blood directly to that part of him he was desperately trying to ignore. He wanted a seduction, not a quickie. Taking her hair into his left hand, he wrapped the dark strands around his fist and tugged confidently but gently, a sign to her he was in control. Her mewling noises nearly had him saying to hell with the slow seduction but the little voice in the back of his head told him it would be more meaningful to them both if he took his time.

Gently sucking on the throbbing tendon in her neck, Emmet reveled in her response to him. She threw her hands over her head to the back of his neck and held him in place. A gentle tug on her hair reminded her, she was at his mercy, but his body responded to her far faster than he expected, and it made him dizzy with anticipation.

Finally, he pulled back and released his grip on her hair. She moaned her disappointment and turned to face him. Her usually light eyes were dilated to nearly black and her pink cheeks were an alluring shade, but he took a step back and waited. She took three deep breaths and the side of his mouth ticked up. She would have a hickey before too long at the site where his mouth had played.

Without words, he moved toward the kitchen and found the bottle of wine he wanted from the wine rack above the counter. Two glasses followed and soon he had the cork on the counter and poured. Mara leaned against the doorway watching him. He offered her one of the glasses and, without dropping her gaze, clinked his glass to hers. Before he could change his mind and take her upstairs, he went to the reusable grocery bag they had used on their one stop on the way. Pulling out the groceries, he watched her through the corner of his eye. Soon, a promising smile lifted the corner of her lips. Without words, she pushed off the kitchen archway and headed back to their bags by the entry.

For the life of him, Emmet wanted to step out of the kitchen to see what she was doing. Instead, he busied himself with the groceries. They had chosen specific foods that were easy to prepare. Cheeses, smoked salmon, pre-cut cold meats, olives, fruits and vegetables, and of course, chocolate for dessert.

Setting things out on platters, he pulled out his surprise bottle of champagne. Finding a bucket, he filled it with ice and set it on the counter with two glasses garnished with strawberries. He then went to light the fire in the living room. Checking the time, she had been upstairs for nearly twenty minutes. He was about to go up to find her when her step sounded on the stair. He looked up from the flames and immediately felt the rush of his blood pounding in his ears. Heat from more than the fire rose to his face.

Mara stood in a Bohemian backless, white satin nightgown that pooled at her feet. The front halter had a deep cut from the lace collar to just below her sternum and a bit of red lace was visible between her breasts showing a halter lace Teddy underneath. She had let her hair out from the ponytail and curled the tips. The soft curls fell in mahogany layers around her shoulders. Her eyes were enhanced by liner, mascara and a dark grey smoky eyeshadow. Her lips were ruby red and every part of her face looked flawless.

In short, she looked stunning.

Emmet appreciated all women, with or without makeup, curvy or thin, what he loved was a confident woman and the woman who stood before him was sexy as hell. The soft smile showed she like his appreciative stare.

"Any more of that wine?" Heaven help him, even her voice had dropped to a seductive timbre. He was having a very difficult time reminding himself why it was a good idea to wait.

He nodded and motioned to the champagne. Her eyes lit and she nodded. He popped the cork and poured. She walked over to him and he noticed she was taller than usual. He caught himself hoping against hope she would drop the nightgown and stand before him in the Teddy and heels. Bloody Hell, how was he supposed to get through dinner?

"Thank you," she said.

"You're welcome," he breathed. A smile spread slowly across her ruby red lips. Keeping his gaze, she raised the champagne flute and took a drink. "Dinner?" he got out, indicating the spread of food he had prepared.

"Famished," she answered turning away and walking to the high-top table in the corner. Gracefully sitting, she crossed her legs. The white satin careened down her long legs and god help him, her red high heels peeked out from beneath, expertly matching her lips, nails and the tantalizing bit of Teddy he could see.

Emmet carried the food over and then two plates, taking his seat opposite her. Her finger rimmed the flute as she watched him. He filled her plate then his. They ate in silence for a few minutes until he looked up to see her staring at him.

"What?" he finally asked.

"I have to say I'm impressed."

"Impressed?"

"At the level of your resistance," she admitted.

"Don't be," he replied refilling her champagne glass. "I've already thought of about a dozen ways in this room alone to make you scream my name."

"Then tell me..." she leaned forward. "What are you

waiting for?"

"I have no idea," he admitted.

"Neither do I," she replied. Standing, she offered her hand to him just like he had done earlier. Swallowing audibly, Emmet slid from the chair and took her hand. She smiled softly. Lifting their intertwined hands, she turned and placed his fingers on the back halter of her outfit. The neck was held by two snaps, a quick tug and they would be undone. His gaze went to the food and his last-ditch effort to take things slowly. His decision made, he pulled his eyes back to Mara's neck. With his left hand, he caressed the exposed skin of her back all the way to the curve of her backside. He wondered for a moment if the back of the nightgown showed her bareback, how was the teddy attached? The answer within his grasp, he popped the clasp at her neck, and she turned back to him. The nightgown pooled at her feet and she stood in the sexiest red teddy he had ever seen. The halter was held in place behind the nightgown and the back-crisscrossing ribbons were low enough they had not been visible beneath the gown. The see-through lace at her front drew his attention.

"See something you like there, O'Quinn?"

"Aye," he breathed.

"I hoped so," she said. Taking his hand, she placed it on her lace covered chest. "Still want to have dinner?"

He shook his head. "I'm thinking dessert."

"So was I," she answered. "Take me to bed, Emmet."

"Aye love, it would be my pleasure." They turned together and headed for the stairs.

Emmet woke the next morning to his phone ringing. Mara moaned and turned away from him. He grinned at the memory of the night before. But before he could remember everything in full detail, and possibly reenact parts of it, he answered the call.

"Emmet, glad I caught you," his solicitor said.

"Morning, what can I do for you?" Emmet asked.

"I received the court date and didn't want to wait to tell you. It's Tuesday."

"Tuesday?" he questioned. "But I thought they would give us a week's notice."

"Normally yes, but because Trevor's grandparents wanted to fly back to the States by the twenty-first, the court agreed to push up the date to the next available. Tuesday at three. I wanted to go over a couple last minute things with you. Could you meet me at my office at noon?"

"I'm actually in Sligo for the weekend," Emmet said.

"Oh, all right, well, first thing Monday then. We need to go over a few questions the judge with ask."

"Yeah, sure. I'll be there."

"Grand, see you then."

"Yeah, see you then," Emmet hung up the phone and looked over at Mara. She had woken and was watching him. "Good morning," he said.

"Good morning," she answered.

"That was not the way I intended to wake you up this morning."

She grinned and snuggled into the pillow, closed her eyes and said, "I'm asleep again. Wake me how you would have."

Emmet chuckled and slowly stroked her bare side all the way down to her knee and back up again then leaned over to her and kissed his way down her neck to her chest then down further until she couldn't stop her moaned; "Emmet."

"I'm glad you still can say my name after all the times you screamed it last night," he teased.

She popped one eye open and looked at him then the other eye opened and she ran her fingers through his hair. He hummed a happy sigh.

"I'll always say it, Em," she said. "I love you."

A soft surprised smile lit his face. "Mara, I love you too."

She leaned forward and kissed him. Soon, they both lost themselves in each other's bodies.

CHAPTER
TWENTY-ONE

Emmet lazily hummed as he stroked Mara's back as her head rested on his chest. Kissing the top of her head, he eased his arm out from under her and swung his legs over the side of the bed.

"Where are you going?" she asked.

"I don't know about you, love, but I'm starving," he said. "I didn't get a chance to eat last night and it's nearly ten. I want my breakfast."

"Oh of course," she teased. "Don't let me get in the way of my growing man and his food."

He turned to her and gestured to his abs, all eight of them. "Damn right. I'm thinking I'll just lie around, maybe have some junk food on Sundays while watching the telly. Dad bod, here I come."

"You know..." she started, raising to her elbows for a better view. "I'm pretty sure I'd love you if you had an eight pack, a dad bod, or a beer belly. I love *you*, Emmet O'Quinn, not your body."

Emmet paused as he was pulling on his sweatpants. It was the first time she said those words. Though he knew it, it was nice to hear. It was more than nice. He wanted to hear those words every day for the rest of his life. Looking over at her, an idea niggled from the back of his mind. Before he could stop himself, the words were tumbling out. "Marry me, Mara."

"What?" Mara asked surprised.

No going back now, he thought and knelt on one knee. "I love you," he said confidently. "Will you marry me?" he asked. "I want to spend the rest of my days by your side. I don't have a ring, but I will. I want to be your husband and make every dream of yours a reality."

"Emmet."

"I'm not crazy, nor drunk. I am completely sober like I was last night when I had the best night of my life. I want that for the rest of my days. I love you. I always have and I always will. Be my wife, Mara. Let me proclaim to the world you are mine and I am yours."

"Emmet..."

She searched his gaze for any indication he was teasing her but when she found none, she grinned widely and nodded. "Yes. Yes, Emmet. I will marry you, gladly!"

Emmet let out a breath, laughed in disbelief and whooped in excitement. He tackled her to the bed, eliciting a fit of giggles from her that quickly turned into moans of pleasure. He had his wife, now to have his son with him too and his world would be complete.

As soon as Emmet opened the door of his parent's house back in Kerry, he took a deep breath. Mara had not stopped twisting her engagement ring. She loved Victorian styles and when they ventured out to Sligo Town for lunch, they stopped in to an antique store. When she saw the ring under the case, Emmet knew it was the one. At his urging, she tried it on and when it fit, he immediately looked at the older man behind the counter. He smiled and nodded. Emmet knelt to one knee again, right there in the store.

"Mara McGrath, you already said yes this morning, but now you have a proper ring. So, I'll ask you again. Will you marry me?" He asked.

Tears gathered in her eyes as she looked at the ring on her finger and then at Emmet. She nodded. "Yes, Emmet. Again, yes!"

A small crowd had gathered and all clapped when he rose to his feet and kissed her. After he paid for the ring, she never took it off and he caught her staring at it randomly with a soft smile all the way back to Kerry. When they had stopped for a quick snack, Emmet called his stepmother and asked her to gather everyone together. He had an announcement to make. Hoping she would think it was about Trevor and the hearing, he thanked her when she promised to call everyone. Now the time had come for him to not only tell his family about the court date but also about getting married.

As soon as they were through the door, Emmet looked around. Everyone was there. His parents, his brothers and their wives, his sister, Ness's mom and Dermott, her husband. His Aunt Siobhan and cousin Keera from Clare, and even Tom and Chloe. Mara went to her sister and gave her a hug, then immediately back to Emmet in the middle of the room and took his hand.

They were all quiet, waiting for Emmet to speak. Looking at each of them individually, he sighed.

"Thank you all for being here," he began. "As you know, Mara and I drove up to Sligo yesterday and stayed over at the cottage. We intended to stay tonight too, but I received a call from my solicitor this morning. For those of you who do not know," he looked at Chloe. "I was approached by letter from a woman I knew briefly about four years ago. She told me she had a son and she was dying. She claimed the lad was mine."

Chloe's eyes grew wide as she looked up at Tom then over at Mara.

"I had a paternity test done," at that point he looked at his father who nodded encouragingly. "He is mine." The women in his family gasped, their hands flying to either their mouths or hearts. "I've known for a couple weeks. I didn't tell you as soon as I found out because I didn't want you to get your hopes up. The reason I'm telling you all now is because, I received the court date and also, this beautiful woman..." he looked down at Mara then to Chloe who took Tom's hand that rested on her shoulder. "Mara," he turned back to her. "Has agreed to stand by me through it all. She has agreed to be my wife."

Everything erupted at once. His stepmother and Ness squealed and rushed to him. Mara was grabbed by her sister and held tightly. Emmet couldn't hear what she said to her, but they were both smiling through their tears. Tom and his brothers pulled him into a back-slapping hug, but his father cupped his face and stared into his eyes for a long moment then embraced him tightly.

"Congratulations, my boy," he whispered. "I have waited for this day and I know your mother is looking down, smiling at your choice."

"Thank you, da'," Emmet replied.

"I love you," he pulled back and kissed his cheek.

"I love you too," Emmet answered and squeezed his father's shoulder.

"When is the wedding?" Deirdre came up to them.

"We haven't decided that yet," Mara said. "But I would like Spring? We want to get through the hearing first and get Trevor acclimated to his new world, then..."

"So, when is the court date?" Sean asked.

"Tuesday," Emmet replied. "We have agreed to tell no one else about our engagement until after the hearing."

"Of course, oh sweetheart, I'm so happy for you!" Deirdre gushed.

"Thank you, ma," he said. His aunt pushed her way through and gave him a big hug. Then his cousin Keera, who looked much paler than normal came up to him and forced a smile.

"Congratulations, Em," she said softly.

"Cheers, Kee, you all right?" he asked.

She gave the worst forced nod he'd ever seen and when she turned away, he swore he saw tears in her eyes. But before he could do much more than wonder, his mother had grabbed both he and his fiancée and pulled them away.

"Let's get some food in you and talk wedding prep," Deirdre said.

She hurried them to the kitchen table, then she went about the kitchen pulling out food and dishes with the help of her daughters-in-law except for Ness who went up to Emmet and hugged him tightly.

"I am so happy for you," she mumbled into his chest.

"Thank you, love," he stroked her back. When she pulled away, she wiped her tears and smiled at him, kissing his cheek.

"Stupid hormones," she laughed then looked at Mara. "You know you are getting one of the best men I know. You take care of him."

"I love him, Ness, I promise I will," Mara stated and gave her a hug.

Orin came out of the kitchen with a tray of champagne glasses, some filled more than others as the women who were pregnant; Ness and Chloe, could only have a single sip. As they toasted to Emmet's and Mara's happiness, Emmet took a moment to look around the room as he pulled his fiancée into his side. He only needed one other person there to make his world complete and he hoped and prayed that by the end of Tuesday, his son would be with him.

CHAPTER
TWENTY-TWO

The morning of the court hearing, Emmet woke from only a light sleep much earlier than he needed. He hadn't slept much that night, his stomach in knots all evening. Mara was fast asleep beside him and he smiled. Staring at his fiancée, a thought entered his mind and as much as he told himself it was a bad idea, he couldn't shake the feeling it was right. The idea was there to stay and the more he thought about it, the more he tried to figure out how to do it. Sliding away from her, he took his computer from the chair where he left it the night before. Sitting at the breakfast table in his apartment, he opened the laptop and keyed in his search.

Thirty minutes later, his stomach was again in knots but for an entirely different reason. Having made plans with his eldest brother Cabhan, he poured a cup of coffee and added it to a tray along with a few slices of sausage, two eggs and toast. Carrying the tray to the bedroom, he locked eyes with Mara who had just woken up.

"I smell sausage and coffee," she said.

He smiled and indicated the tray. She stretched in bed, arching her body back and putting her arms above her head. The sheets pulled down, revealing the curves that made his mouth water. Setting the tray on the nightstand, he crawled across the bed and growled as he took her lips in a rough kiss. She kissed him back but never opened her mouth, no matter how much coaxing Emmet tried.

Finally, she pulled back and pressed her lips together, Emmet raised an eyebrow.

"Morning breath," she mumbled. He laughed out right.

"Well before you go brush, have a sip of coffee. It always tastes better before the minty baking soda taste," he offered her a mug.

"Breakfast in bed? What did I do to earn such devotion?"

"Should I avoid talking about sex here?" Emmet teased.

Mara giggled but took a sip, moaning at the taste. Emmet's lips followed the coffee mug and he kissed her again.

"I'm the only one who is allowed to make you moan like that," he said.

"You'll have to share with coffee."

"Anything else I'll have to share with?"

She pretended to think about it. "Coffee... wine, whiskey, scones, scotch eggs, pizza," Emmet cut her off with a hard kiss.

"Tease," he replied when he pulled back. She eyed him and raised her coffee mug to her lips again.

"What do you have on your mind?" she asked after a moment. "I see something behind your eyes. Are you worried about the hearing? It'll be fine. I'll be right there. So will your whole family."

"It's not that, love," he said pulling away and reclining in the bed, propped up by his elbow.

"Then what is it?"

Emmet looked away for a second, then back into her eyes. "I may have... set an appointment."

"What kind of appointment?"

Taking a deep breath, Emmet plunged ahead. "I don't want to wait until Spring to make you my wife. They have an opening an hour before the hearing at the courthouse. Cabhan has agreed to be our witness, but I want to make you mine. Marry me... today."

"You mean..." Mara began. "Marry you at the courthouse, today?"

Emmet nodded. "I don't want to tell anyone. Cabhan agreed to be a witness. I just need to tell him you said yes. I'll tell everyone, shout it from the rooftops as soon as the hearing is over. But I cannot wait any longer to make you my wife. I promise when this is all over, we will have a proper wedding reception, a *Céilí*, whatever you want. Do you agree? Or have I scared you off properly?"

Mara stared at him for a long moment. "Yes," she finally said.

"Which one?" Emmet asked.

"Yes, I agree. Let's get married!" She exclaimed excitedly.

"Really?" Emmet questioned. When she nodded, he let out an excited shout and grabbed her to him, kissing her deeply. The breakfast and even the coffee forgotten, they lay back and loved each other until Emmet's alarm rang.

Rushing around, they each took a shower separately, knowing if they took one together, they would never make it on time. Mara quickly put on some makeup, making Emmet promise that once the hearing was over, they would plan a proper wedding so she could get a wedding dress and have her hair and makeup done professionally. He would have promised her anything at that moment and soon they were rushing out the door and into his car.

Cabhan was waiting for them at the courthouse, in a suit,

one of the few times Emmet had seen his brother in a three piece.

"Thought you guys wouldn't make it," he said as they hurried up the steps.

"We're here," Emmet replied embracing his brother. "You didn't tell anyone?"

"No one knows," he confirmed. "Rachael thought I was going to pay respects to mum's grave, which I did so it wasn't a lie."

"Thank you," Emmet breathed.

"You're welcome," Cabhan looked over at Mara in a light-yellow sun dress. "You look lovely. I stopped to get some flowers for mum's grave and thought you might not have time," he offered a small bouquet of red roses and baby's breath. "So, I picked up another bouquet."

"Oh Cabhan, thank you," she breathed, taking the flowers and a deep sniff.

"My pleasure," he replied.

Music struck up behind them as street performers began playing a song. "Oh, do we have two extra minutes?" she begged. "*Raglan Road* is my favorite."

Emmet looked at his watch. "For you? Anything." Mara held Emmet's hand as they listened and soon the town clock struck the top of the hour and the band ended the song.

Cabhan placed a hand on both of their shoulders, "come on, they can't marry you out here."

Since both Emmet and Mara had agreed not to tell anyone about their marriage and due to how fast everything had happened, Mara hadn't had a chance to get Emmet a ring, but she kept her engagement ring on. Excitement raced through her as she planned to go after the hearing and find her husband a ring to proclaim that man was hers. Having heard her favorite song on the way in to be married, she took it as a blessing and a sign she had done the right thing. She couldn't contain her grin as she sat beside Cabhan on the aisle pew of the courtroom. Emmet's entire family sat next to, in front of and behind her, but her eyes were zeroed in to her husband's back as he stood with his solicitor and barrister, talking at their table. Emmet nodded at something the other man said but turned when he must have felt her eyes on him. He smiled at her then turned around fully when the door opened and his son was carried into the room by an older man, his wife beside him.

"Daddy," the little boy exclaimed seeing him and Emmet's smile took her breath away.

"Trev!" Emmet called out.

"Daddy!" he said again and squirmed out of the older man's arms. When the grandfather set him down, Trevor rushed to Emmet who had crouched down, his arms outstretched to him. He picked his son up and twirled him around. The little boy giggled uncontrollably. Emmet held him close and the little boy threw his arms around his neck.

Seeing Trevor for the first time, Mara understood why Emmet knew before the paternity test he was his son. Trevor's auburn hair was the exact same shade as his and his piercing blue eyes were clearly inherited from the boy's father. Emmet's eyes found her, and she could do nothing but smile.

She couldn't hear what Emmet said to his son, but the boy nodded and started telling him about the big animals he saw at the Dublin Zoo. Finally, the older couple walked over to them. Emmet nodded in greeting. "Joann, Curtis."

The man said nothing, but the woman smiled warmly at him. "Emmet," she replied. "It's good to see you. I'm sorry it's under these circumstances."

"I'm not, Joann, any way I can see my son is a good circumstance," Emmet confided and teasingly tweaked Trevor's nose causing the little boy to giggle again. "I just hope, no matter the outcome of today we will share him?"

"Of course!" Joann replied but Curtis grunted.

"Planning on moving to America?" Curtis demanded. "That's the only way you'll see him *when* we win."

"Curtis," Joann scolded.

Emmet's jaw ticked but his solicitor put a hand on his shoulder.

"We should talk before the judge arrives," he said. Emmet nodded and looked at his son.

"I'll see you when this is all over, *mo leanbh*," Emmet said calling his son the Irish name for *my child*.

Trevor threw his arms around Emmet's neck. "I love you, daddy." Emmet closed his eyes and hugged him.

"I love you too, son."

Finally, Emmet let his son down and watched as he walked to his aunt, Trevor's mother's sister. The woman nodded in greeting to Emmet but took Trevor's hand and walked him out of the courtroom.

The grandparents went to their table where their solicitor and barrister waited as Emmet turned back to the two men beside him.

"So long as you've followed my advice, this should be easy," his solicitor said.

Mara held her breath as Emmet glanced back at her. Fortunately, they did not have long to wait. The judge was announced and the middle-aged woman sat at the bench.

Chapter
Twenty-Three

Both barristers presented their arguments, both strong cases in Mara's opinion. The grandparents claimed that if their daughter had wanted Emmet to know about their son, she would have told him sooner. Mara noticed Joann said very little at that point and it made her wonder. Emmet's case was, he had a right to know regardless, as he was the biological father and had not waived his rights. Emmet's barrister also presented Trevor's mother's letter to Emmet and her Last Will and Testament where she named Emmet as Trevor's sole guardian. The judge listened, asked questions about Emmet's career and stability as well as the grandparent's age, income and homelife. She was clearly impartial, and Mara breathed a little easier.

Finally, Emmet's philandering was brought up and Mara bit her lip. She saw the guilt in Emmet's posture. His solicitor leaned over and whispered something in his ear. Emmet nodded and sat up straighter with his hands on the arms of the chair, very open and approachable body language. When the judge looked at him, he met her gaze, unwavering.

"What is your response to this, Mr. O'Quinn?" She asked.

"Your honor," he stood and addressed her. "It is true, in my past I have been known as a philanderer. I'm not denying that, but I can say I am happy I *was* that way because if I wasn't, I wouldn't have that little boy. I know the grandparents are trying to paint me as a reckless lover, but I assure you, I am not that way anymore. I love that little boy and I would do anything to be given the chance to be his father."

"That seems reasonable," she replied, then looked back at the grandparents. "Rebuttal?"

"At this time, I would ask the courts to take a look at these photos," the grandparent's barrister said accepting a large envelope from the solicitor. "I believe this will clear up the little matter of *if* his behavior has indeed changed or not." The barrister handed the envelope to the attendant and Mara's heartbeat sped up. "These are photographs taken just Saturday night of Mr. O'Quinn. He was in a cottage in Sligo with a woman who has not yet been identified but clearly another of his weekend escapades. If he truly has changed, he would not have jumped into bed with yet another woman, let alone try to cover it up by visiting a remote cottage by the sea."

Mara gasped as Emmet collapsed back into his chair and turned a horror filled gaze to her.

"How were these photos obtained?" the judge asked looking through them.

"Knowing Mr. O'Quinn's reputation, my clients, at their solicitor's insistence, hired a private investigator," the barrister went on. "They hoped he truly had changed his ways but, unfortunately they cannot give their grandson to a man who not only sleeps around, but sneaks around."

Mara's ears were ringing as she met and held her husband's gaze. She had cost him his child. Tears streamed down her cheeks. Emmet's barrister was saying something, but Mara couldn't hear anything apart from the rushing of her blood in her ears. Emmet's solicitor patted his shoulder and Emmet turned to see the judge looking at him, expectantly. Taking a breath so deep, his shoulders fell a good inch when he let it out.

"I'll repeat the question, Mr. O'Quinn," the judge said, no discrimination in her tone, only stern focus. "What is your explanation for these photos?"

Slowly Emmet stood, he wobbled for a moment, but his solicitor helped him with a hand on his back.

"Your honor," his voice was tight and soft. He cleared his throat and began again. "Your honor. My explanation is..." he paused. "I... fell in love. The woman in those photos is Mara McGrath. She is in the audience now. I knew her when we were both much younger and I have loved her ever since. I knew Curtis and Joann had hired a private investigator in order to paint me as a player, but the truth is, I have been in love with her for twenty years. And when she returned to Ireland, it did not take long for us to rekindle the flames that never went out. In fact... I apologize, when I first said her name, I named her Mara McGrath, but actually as of this morning, she is Mara O'Quinn, my wife. We were married in the courthouse today down the hall. So, if loving my wife is what costs me to lose my son, well... I do not believe God, nor you nor Curtis and Joann would ever be that cruel. Yes, I was a player. Yes, I slept around and yes, I knew what it could do to me, but as soon as I met my son, I wanted something I never wanted before. To be a father. I love him and my wife more than words can say, and I would never, ever want to harm either of them for any reason.

"We kept it a secret because I knew how it could look, but if loving my wife costs me the other thing I love more than life itself, then so be it. But let me ask you, your honor, have you ever loved with such a love that nothing, no one, and no time could ever remotely change, alter or make you forget that person? That is what Mara O'Quinn is to me. And my son... my son is the reason I am here today, not my love life, not my family but that little boy who means more to me than life itself. That is why I am here. To be given the chance I was denied, to see my son grow and be a father to him, *the* father, no one else can claim to be."

The entire courtroom was silent after Emmet's speech. Cabhan had grabbed Mara's hand and held it comfortingly. The judge had not dropped Emmet's gaze but finally, she leaned back in her chair, looked past Emmet's shoulder and found Mara. Mara tried to wipe the tears. The judge then looked over at Curtis and Joann. Curtis did not raise his gaze, but Joann had tears pooling in her eyes. Even the solicitor looked ashamed.

"Response?" the judge asked. Joann silenced the barrister by standing and addressing the court.

"Your honor, forgive me for speaking out of turn," she began, the judge gestured for her to continue. "Emmet has proven time and time again how much of a gentleman, a good father, son and brother he is. When my daughter first found out she was pregnant, she was overjoyed and called her sister and me immediately. She always wanted to be a mother. She knew who the father was without a doubt as she had just gotten out of a relationship a year before going to Ireland and had not been with anyone else but Emmet. She told her sister and me about this auburn haired, handsome Irishman who made her feel like a queen. She said her one regret was she couldn't stay with him longer but was excited to tell him about their child. Not expecting anything from him but wanting him to be part of his son's life. It was my husband and I who told her not to and I regret it to this day.

"When Trevor was born, we were so happy, but she knew something was missing in his life and had the one picture she had of she and Emmet O'Quinn printed. A selfie taken at a pub in Killarney. I have it here." She pulled out a frame and showed the court. Mara saw Emmet's laughing blue eyes as he grinned for the picture and the woman beside him, a pretty blonde who wore a beanie hat. "Every night, she told Trevor a story about his father, sharing this photo so he would know his father if ever he saw him.

"When she received the diagnosis a year and half later, she wasn't upset, nor worried for herself, she was worried Trevor would never know his father. She made me promise... even my husband doesn't know this... she made me promise to mail the letter to him and to tell Trevor a story of Emmet every night. She had written them down so I knew what to say. My beautiful daughter," she turned the photo around and stroked her daughter's face. "Died, seven months ago and every night I would tell her son a story about his father. But, your honor," tears streamed down her cheeks as her voice cracked and she shrugged. "I've run out of stories. And I think my daughter would say, it's time for Emmet to tell their son his own stories." She looked over at him and smiled. "He will be a wonderful father and husband and I pray he will be generous with his son and allow us to see him."

"Are you forfeiting your rights?" the judge asked.

"I am," she whimpered as more tears rained down her cheeks. "Because that is what my daughter would want."

After a long pause, the judge cleared her throat and the tell-tale simmer in her eyes. "So be it. I do not see why full custody cannot be granted to the father, Emmet O'Quinn. Case dismissed." She hit the gavel and for a moment nothing happened, no one moved, no one spoke, they didn't even breathe but as soon as she stood and left the room, the entire public section exploded in cheers. Emmet jumped, not expecting the noise and his solicitor slapped him on the back. He shook hands with the barrister and thanked him but then his eyes went to Joann and he mouthed *thank you.* Mara saw Joann nod to him and then the doors opened and Trevor rushed in.

"Trev!" Emmet shouted.

"Daddy!" he exclaimed and launched himself into Emmet's arms. "Aunt Charlotte said I get to go home with you, is that true?"

"It is, big man, if you want," he said.

"Yes, yes yes!" he wiggled and threw his arms around him. "I love you, daddy."

"I love you too," Emmet held his son tighter to him and search the crowd. Mara met his gaze and he reached one arm toward her. She raced to him and wrapped her arms around his waist.

"I love you," she cried happy tears.

"I love you," he answered and kissed her thoroughly. Trevor gave a cute disgusted sound and they pulled back. "Trevor, this is Mara. She's my wife and your stepmom."

"Hi," he said softly.

"Hello, it's so wonderful to meet you, Trevor. Your daddy has told me a lot about you."

"You talk just like my daddy," he said. "Your voice is funny." He giggled when Mara tickled his tummy.

"Emmet," Joann's voice came from behind them. She stood demurely waiting. Emmet turned to speak to her.

"Joann, thank you," he said. "And never fear, you and Curtis can see him anytime you want. I would never stop you and I'd love to see America. Maybe Mara and I can go there for our honeymoon."

"We'd love to have you. Both," she looked at Mara. "Can I say goodbye?" She indicated Trevor.

"No," Emmet breathed. "Not goodbye, never goodbye."

She nodded but accepted Trevor into her arms when Emmet handed him over.

"Gramma, why are you crying?" Trevor asked. Giving them a moment alone, Emmet and Mara turned to his family, waiting. He saw the looks on his stepmother's and Ness's faces.

"I'm in trouble," he teased.

"Aye, I think we both are," Mara giggled.

"Well then, wife, let's face them the same way we'll do everything... together," he said.

"Together, Em, absolutely," she took his hand and they stepped toward his family.

Emmet could hardly believe his good fortune, he had his wife on his right and his son in his arms. Life was good. Orin offered to take everyone out to dinner, Curtis and Joann included so they could get to know one another. He thanked his lucky stars his father and Deirdre were so outgoing and accepting of Curtis and Joann. Orin found common ground with Curtis talking about fishing and Deirdre was ecstatic to learn Joann was a baker.

As they all headed out of the courthouse, Emmet pulled Mara closer to him. They stopped at the top of the outdoor steps for a kiss, his family cheering.

The steps were busy with people coming and going and Emmet cautiously held his son tighter in his arms as he started down the stairs.

So focused on the stone steps and making sure he didn't trip, he did not see the man walking up toward them until the man shouted to Mara;

"I told you I would take everything from you, just like you took everything from me!"

Emmet's eyes flashed up to the man. Before he could think, the man pulled out a gun, aimed, and two loud shots rang out.

Emmet didn't feel them at first, but the world began to tilt. Screams were all around him, but as the stone steps grew closer, his one thought was his son. Hoping against hope Trevor would be all right, Emmet held him tightly to his chest as his back crashed onto the stone. Trevor was crying and yelling his name but soon he was scooped up by Curtis. The grandfather would take care of him. But why was Emmet on the ground, and more importantly why was he in pain?

So much pain.

His chest was going to collapse, he was sure of it. He couldn't breathe. He couldn't move, all he could hear were screams and then Mara's face appeared over him.

"Emmet!" She screamed. "Stay with me, stay with me. Please god, stay with me."

"T-T-T-Tre-Trev-Trev-"

"He's fine," she hurriedly said. "Stay with me. Please."

His son was fine, that's all he needed to hear. Weakly, he raised his hand, seeing blood on his fingers, but he didn't care, Mara looked so scared. He had to reassure her. Cupping her face, he smiled when she held on to his wrist and covered his hand with hers.

"No no no no no, stay with me. Don't you dare die!"

"I... love... you," he breathed out.

"Emmet! No! Please!" was all he heard before everything went black.

CHAPTER
TWENTY-FOUR

"Let me through!" Cabhan shouted as he worked through the crowd to his brother.

Mara was screaming for Emmet to stay with her. Cabhan raced down the steps, ripped off his suit jacket and pressed it to his brother's chest.

All Mara could do was hold Emmet's hand and stare at his face. His eyes were closed but there was so much blood.

"I told you what I would do! I told you!" the sound of Ben's voice shook her out of her thoughts. He had been on the steps and she never saw him until it was too late. Dear god. He had just killed her husband. She didn't see Cabhan working nor the Gardaí and paramedics rushing the scene. All she saw was Emmet. Something snapped and she looked over at the man who had just taken the life of the man she loved. She felt an all-consuming anger and screamed. Taking off toward Benjamin as the Gardaí were cuffing him on one of the stair landings, she didn't think, she only ran. Slamming into him, she grabbed his waist in a tackle hold and used their momentum to career down the steps. She didn't feel anything as they hit the stone. When they came to a thudding stop, she didn't think, she only threw punch after punch. She didn't feel, all she saw was Emmet's blood and the man beneath her had caused it.

Two Garda tried to pull her off him, but she kept beating his face into the stone. She didn't know what she was saying to him, but she kept hitting him over and over and over again. Her love, her best friend, her husband was dead, and it was her fault. It was all her fault.

Finally, the police pulled her off Ben. She crawled away as pain and tears assaulted her body. She screamed, her cheek resting against the cool of the stone, her eyes on the paramedics and Cabhan working around Emmet. Tom's arms came gently around her shoulders and turned her to him. She clung to him as she watched her lover being carried on a gurney into an ambulance.

"He's alive, Mara," she heard Tom say. "He's alive."

Looking up at her brother-in-law, she couldn't believe he would hurt her. Emmet was dead, she saw it herself. Tom would hurt her? *Never.* Some unconscious thought screamed. Tom would never hurt her.

"He's alive?" she questioned.

"Aye, he's alive," Tom replied. He didn't say the words *for now,* but they were both thinking them. It was chaos on the steps, but Mara's mind couldn't comprehend anything except her husband was alive. But she could have caused him to almost lose, not only his life, but his son's as well. Nothing would change until Ben was in prison... or dead. Emmet wouldn't be safe if she stayed with him so long as Ben was still around. She couldn't risk it. She couldn't risk being with Emmet. She had to give him up.

Emmet didn't know what was going on, all he felt was an

ache in his chest and a listlessness in his limbs. His eyes were heavy, he could barely open them. With considerable effort, he finally pushed his eye lids back and looked around the room. Cabhan sat in the chair by the bed looking down at a file in his hand.

Trying to speak, he could only grunt around the breathing tube down his throat. Cabhan immediately looked over and rushed to his side.

"Em," he breathed. "Oh, thank god. Easy, easy, let me get the tube out."

Cabhan tried to remove the tube gently but Emmet still gagged and the pain that assaulted his body caused him to temporarily stop breathing.

"Easy," Cabhan's voice was the same calm tone Emmet had heard him use with a broodmare when she was in labor. As village vet, Cabhan was the only doctor of anything in the village and was used to dealing with both people and animals.

"What happened?" Emmet finally asked when he got his breath back. Last he remembered, he was holding Trevor and Mara. Trevor. His eyes grew wide as he remembered falling while holding his son.

"Trevor? Where is he? Is he okay?" Emmet tried to get up.

"Don't move," Cabhan ordered.

"Where's my son?"

"He's fine. He's with Curtis and Joann outside, just there," he indicated the door to Emmet's right.

"What about Mara? What happened?" Emmet begged.

"You were shot twice in the chest by a man named Benjamin Taylor. He was Mara's old boss in London. She told us everything."

"Did they get him?" Emmet asked.

"Aye, your wife knocked him down some steps and beat

the shite out of him," Cabhan said.

"But she's all right?"

"As far as I know, she's fine. A little banged up from falling down the stairs, but I haven't seen her."

"Where is Trevor? Where am I? Can I see him? And Mara?"

"You're in the hospital, Trevor is outside with his grandparents, let me call the nurse and aye, I'll let them in."

Cabhan left his side and opened the door. A muffled conversation was all Emmet heard before Curtis and Joann entered, holding Trevor.

"Daddy!" Trevor cried his little face red with tears.

"Hey big man," he breathed and reached for him.

"Easy, Trevor," Curtis said as he brought him closer. "He wants to hug you, but I don't think that's a good idea," his eyes went to the IV tubes and EKG hookups.

Emmet nodded. "I'm all right, Trev." Emmet raised a weak hand to caress his son's soft arm.

"I was so scared, Daddy," Trevor said.

"I'm so sorry, *mo leanbh*. I didn't mean to scare you."

Trevor nodded but took his father's hand. "Will you be all right?"

"Och, aye, you'll see. I'll be fine. Promise."

Trevor nodded and fiddled with a Rosary around his neck. "Gramma Dee gave me this," he said. Emmet looked to Curtis and Joann for clarification.

"Deirdre," Joann confirmed.

"She said if I prayed really hard you would be okay. And you're okay! I prayed really, really hard."

"Thank you, big man," Emmet said.

A knock on the door drew everyone's attention. Emmet looked over thinking it was Mara but when Sean and Ness peeked in, his brows furrowed for a second and then he smiled.

"We'll leave you," Joann said softly as she leaned down and gave him a small hug. "Thank you for protecting Trevor." She kissed his cheek.

"Always," Emmet replied.

"Get better soon. We're just out here."

Emmet nodded and watched them leave.

As soon as they were alone, Ness rushed over to Emmet and threw her arms around his neck.

"You can never do that to me again, do you understand?" she demanded.

"Yes, ma'am," he teased. "I'll be sure to mark *Tuesdays, get shot* off my calendar."

She smacked his arm. "Not funny."

"I'm sorry, love," he replied. "I didn't mean to worry you or my nephew." He looked down at her belly, but it was much flatter than he expected. His eyes shot up to hers.

"Seeing you shot and nearly dead..." she shook her head. "I went into labor. He's a fine and healthy lad, thank god. We named him after my father; Liam. Liam... Emmet."

Emmet's chest filled with love and he pulled Ness down for a hug. "Are you all right?"

She nodded. "And now that you're awake I'm even better."

"How long have I been out?"

"About five days," Sean said squeezing his brother's forearm.

"Damn," he breathed. "Where's Mara?" Ness looked at him, then down, shrugged and shook her head. "Where is she, Ness?"

"I don't know. She's... not been here with you at all."

"Is she all right? What happened?"

Ness shook her head again. "She's fine but she won't come see you. I tried to talk to her but she..."

"Doesn't want to," Emmet finished.

Ness nodded. "I'm sorry, Em."

"It's all right," he forced. "Cabhan was looking for a nurse, I think. I'm going to rest again... I'm... I'm tired."

Ness nodded and kissed his cheek. Sean squeezed his hand and they both left the room. Emmet searched his mind. Had he said something to Mara to make her not want to be there? He prayed he hadn't said anything about Chloe by mistake but as hard as he tried, he couldn't remember. Remembering where the morphine control was from his last little visit to the hospital, he found it and ticked it up just enough to give him a chance to sleep pain free, fully aware of his limitations and former addictions.

Closing his eyes, he drifted off to oblivion, still worried about his wife.

CHAPTER TWENTY-FIVE

When next Emmet opened his eyes, movement in front of the window to his left, drew his attention. Mara paced the floor, wringing her hands. She was pale and shaking but she was there... finally.

"Mara," he breathed. She stopped and looked over at him. He wasn't sure what was worse, her nervous pacing or her dead, emotionless eyes.

Moving the bed up with the automatic button, he sat up and reached for her. She took a step back, further away from him. His brows furrowed.

"Are you all right, love?" he asked. She swallowed audibly and turned away from him. "Mara," he said a little more firmly. "What's wrong?"

She started shaking her head and began pacing again. "I'll never forgive myself," she finally said.

"What? What for?" he asked.

"This," she indicated him in the bed.

"I'm fine, love," he answered. "Come here." Again, he reached for her, but she moved even further away. "Mara."

She shook her head. "The man who shot you was Ben. He did it because he swore he would destroy anything and everything I cared about." Her voice worried him. She sounded so cold, so empty. "I'm sorry he thought that was you."

"What are you talking about?" he asked. Her tone told him she wasn't sorry at all.

"I'm saying. I'm sorry you got roped into this. He obviously thought you meant something to me. He was wrong."

"What?" Emmet shook his head trying to process her words.

"I have petitioned the courts not to process our marriage license. They have agreed. We are not officially married until that happens. So... you are free to be Trevor's father without a worry of being married to a woman who really doesn't care about you."

"You're lying."

"I'm not lying. I'm sorry. I thought I wanted this, but I didn't realize I would be an instant mother until it happened. It was eye-opening because if you died, I would have had to take care of him. I can't. I'm sorry. You will not be bothered by me again."

"I love you and I know you love me. You're only saying this because you don't want him to know how much you truly care about me," Emmet stated.

"That's not true. I don't love you. I thought I knew what love was, but I don't, because I've never felt it."

"You are my wife before God. I made vows."

"Maybe, but before the courts we're still free. I'm sorry, Emmet. I enjoyed our time but that's it."

"No, I refuse to believe that," he attempted to get up, but the pain took his breath away.

"Don't go after something that's already gone. Don't embarrass yourself like that Emmet. I hope you and Trevor find the one who is meant for you. Sadly, it's not me. I'm sorry to have led you on but it's over."

"No, no it's not. Mara, you are my wife."

"No, I'm not Emmet. I'm sorry," she rushed to the door, but he swung his legs over the side of the bed, ignoring the searing pain in his chest.

"Mara, don't go."

"I have to," she stated.

"Wait, stop please. Talk to me. I love you!"

She froze at the open door. "I don't love you. Goodbye, Emmet." She left the room.

Emmet tried to stand and go after her, but he could hardly put one foot in front of the other. Something wet slid down his chest. He looked down to see blood seeping onto his hospital gown. "Mara!" He yelled down the hall, but he couldn't walk to the door. Grey mist swirled in front of his eyes. He refused to pass out. He had to go to his wife. She was only saying those things because she thought Ben would hurt him again. He had to tell her he understood and that she was his and he hers. One more step and the pain increased.

"Mara! Wait!" he shouted.

A figure appeared in the doorway and for a second, he thought it was her, but his brother's form came into focus.

"What in the bloody hell are you doing?" Cabhan yelled. "I need help in here!" He shouted down the hall.

"Out of my way," Emmet slurred. "I need to see my wife."

Cabhan blocked his way and caught him when he stumbled.

"You've ripped your stitches, you eejit. Now get back into bed," Cabhan ordered and nearly dragged him back to the hospital bed. A few nurses came running in and helped Cabhan.

"She didn't mean it! Tell me you know she didn't mean it!" Emmet cried.

"All I know is, your wife hasn't been here with you for a single minute of the past five days," Cabhan cut open Emmet's hospital gown for the hospital doctor to better see the ripped stitches.

Emmet grabbed his shoulder. "Please find her."

"I tried. She didn't *want* to be here, Emmet. I'm sorry, but she's not the one for you. She isn't fighting for you. She wasn't here for you."

"No," Emmet fought. "She's scared that's all. Please god, tell me she's only scared."

"I can't tell you that, Em. If she truly loved you, she would be here. And she's not."

Emmet let out a painfilled cry. "Lies! She loves me as I love her!"

"She's torn up your wedding certificate, Em," Cabhan revealed. "I didn't want to tell you. I'm sorry but it's over."

Emmet shook his head, grabbing his brother close and screaming into his shoulder as realization and tears came upon him.

"You are alive, and you have a son who adores you."

Something broke inside him and Emmet leaned back in the hospital bed, numb, allowing the nurses and doctor to seal his stitches again. There was no pain, no joy, he was empty, just a shell. Cabhan stood by the window where Mara had stood not half an hour ago, ripping his dream away from him.

One thing was certain, if he survived this, Emmet would not be able to stay in Ireland. There were too many memories. Seeing Mara in the ditch with her bike on top of her. Playing with her in the ocean when she was just a girl. Seeing her again as she bought her car. Holding her as she cried. Feeling her arms around his middle as they rode on his motorcycle the first time.

Seeing her at Sean's house when he was helping his father with the shed. Seeing her blow a kiss from her room in Tom's house like a randy teenager. Their walk along the beach as they talked. Their first kiss. The first time they made love. When she agreed to be his wife. When she agreed to his hairbrained plan of getting married that day. How she accepted his son and left the courthouse with him. And finally, when she walked out of his life, less than an hour before.

Dear god, she was everywhere. She was in the eyes of his family, his dog, his flat, his parent's cottage, his favorite views, he shared them all with her. Every time he would see them now, he would only be able to feel the pain he felt when she let him. She may have torn up the marriage license, but he had made vows. Forsaking all others. In sickness and in health. Till death. He would never, *could* never break those vows. His wife left him, but she was still his wife.

No, one thing was certain. There were far too many memories in Ireland.

Chapter
Twenty-Six

Four Years Later

"Come on, Daddy! Come on!" Trevor pulled on Emmet's hand as he nearly ran around Military Park in Indianapolis, Indiana. "I can hear the music from here!"

"Aye, so can I, lad," Emmet smiled. "It's called *Carrickfergus.*"

"I want Shepherd's Pie and lemonade, and one of those funny hats and I want to dance, and I want—"

"Whoa there, lad," Emmet laughed. "That's an awful lot of *wants.*"

"But Daddy, you said I could have five things I wanted since it was my birthday last week."

"So I did," Emmet conceded. "Let's get in and find your grandma and granddad. Then we'll talk about which of those *wants* are *likes.*"

Trevor nodded emphatically and pulled on Emmet's

hand. Once through the ticket gate, Emmet held Trevor's hand tighter so he wouldn't run off at the first sight of the Irish Wolfhounds. Those beautiful gentle beasts were his son's favorite part of the festival. After they moved through the crowded front with vendor's tents, the park opened, and Emmet's ears were assaulted by two stages with different bands on opposite sides of the park. Emmet pulled up and turned Trevor to him, crouching down to be eye level with his son, he waited until Trevor stopped looking around and met his eyes.

"You have to promise me you won't go running off, aye?" Trevor nodded. "And if you get separated from any one of us, you find one of the policemen and tell him your name and mine, all right?" He nodded again. "If they ask where you were supposed to meet me, you tell him the main event tent, right in the middle of the park." Emmet indicated the large tent beside them. Trevor nodded again. "And never, ever walk away with any stranger. I don't care if they say I sent them, understand?"

"I promise, Daddy. I won't run off and I'll talk to the police if I get lost. I won't believe any stranger either."

"That's my boy," Emmet winked and ruffled his son's auburn curly hair. "Now let's go find grandma. I think I see your grandad. Come on."

They made their way across the large field to the food tents where Curtis was waiting. Emmet called out and he turned just in time to catch Trevor running to him.

"Oomph," Curtis teased. "There you are! I was getting worried you would miss all the good food since I was going to eat it all."

"You can't eat *all* of it, grandpa," Trevor said looking up at him, his arms still wrapped around his middle. "Grandma wouldn't be happy with you."

"Right you are," he winked then looked up to see Emmet walking up. Swinging an arm around Emmet's shoulders, he gave him a side hug as Trevor had yet to let go. "Get you anything, Em?" Curtis asked.

"Cheers, Guinness for me," Emmet said.

"You have to get your ID checked at the main tent to get a wristband," he showed his.

"Okay. Trev, stay with your grandad."

"Okay," Trevor called after him.

Walking over to the main tent, he stood in line and pulled out his wallet. Due to his son being an American citizen, Emmet had petitioned the courts for an Immediate Relative immigration visa and Curtis and Joann sponsored him. Fortunately, he was able to leave for America only six months after he was shot. Curtis even helped him with employment at his old sales firm. Curtis had retired five years ago but still held sway with some of the hiring managers. It had been three and a half years since Emmet first stepped foot on American soil and so far, he was very glad he did. Ness and Sean had come over a couple times those first two summers since Indianapolis was Ness' hometown. Even though Emmet was happy, he missed his family and Ireland horribly. But after what had happened with Mara, he knew he could not stay in Kerry. He had not seen her since that day in the hospital and something ached with the thought he never would again. Shoving the feeling aside, he embraced the anger he still felt toward her.

He got his wristband and made his way back to the food tents but stopped dead in his tracks when he heard *Raglan Road* being sung by one of the bands. Memories flooded back of he and Mara standing on the steps of the courthouse about to go inside and be married. She was so happy. He was so happy. Then everything changed.

On top of the pain of her betrayal, the subtle kick of homesickness bounced around his chest. Since the first moment Curtis mentioned the Irish Fest, the pang of missing his family and home had grown tenfold. Even though they had been the last three years, for some reason that year was worse than before.

It hurt to breathe, and it hurt to stay listening, but his

feet would not move. He was forced to stay frozen, hearing the words of his wife's favorite song. Hot tears pooled in his eyes as he fought and lost to the pain. Taking deep breath after deep breath, trying to prevent the pain from overpowering him. He looked up to stop the tears but as he closed his eyes, they streamed down his cheeks. Disgusted with his weakness, he tried to shove the pain away, but it was rooted too deep. All he saw was his family and homeland. But when he remembered the ugly dead eyes of his wife as she told him she never loved him, something to this day he refused to believe, the pain receded giving him a moment to breathe. Mara had never tried to contact him in the year after he was shot. He had tried but she refused to see him and he had given up hope. It was much easier to wall off his heart than to think of *what if.*

The song ended and the crowd cheered but Emmet could not stop the pain, it was like he had opened a door and everything came pouring out with no end in sight. Even the next song, a modern pop song with an Irish twist, could not help his longing for home. Looking around, he headed to the portable toilets for some water in the handwashing stations. He couldn't let his son see him like that. Grabbing some paper towels, he pumped water onto them, squeezed out the excess and wiped his face. Pressing the coolness against the back of his neck, he shoved the emotions back behind the mental door, firmly shutting and locking it away. He could breathe easier and with a final push, he placed the invisible mask of happiness he wore, over his face and headed back to his son.

Curtis caught his eye at one of the picnic tables and Emmet headed that way.

"Emmet!" Joann greeted. He placed a hand on her shoulder in greeting.

"Joann, how goes it?"

"Glad you're here," she put an arm around his shoulders as he folded his six-foot-two-inch frame onto the bench and sat beside her.

"Me too," but even to his ears the words were tight.

"Are you all right?" Joann asked.

"Aye, I'm good, cheers, Joann," he said but did not miss the subtle look that passed between Curtis and Joann. Curtis passed him the Guinness and he drank a third of it before he set it down. He needed the beer even if it wasn't nearly as good as it was in Ireland.

"Daddy, I want to go see the dogs," Trevor whined.

"Did you eat your lunch?" Emmet asked.

He nodded emphatically.

"I'll take him," Joann offered.

"You haven't finished," Emmet replied with a forced smile. "No worries, I got him. Come on, big man." He offered his hand to his son. Somewhere in the back of his mind another memory surfaced with that move, but he pushed it back and shook his head. "Remember you cannot go running up to the dogs. Approach slowly and respectfully."

"Yes, Daddy," he agreed, and they walked together.

"We'll catch up with you. Joann wants to look at some of the tents," Curtis called after him.

"I have my mobile," he tossed over his shoulder.

Watching Emmet and Trevor leave the food area, making sure they were out of earshot, Joann leaned into her husband.

"He misses Ireland," she said.

"I thought... hoped this might help. I didn't think it would make things worse," Curtis replied. "I'm sorry."

"You didn't know," she patted her husband's hand. "We've been here several years before. But when was the last time he went out on his own or with people his own age? He's trying so hard to show he's a good father, he's forgotten how to be good to himself. He needs a vacation."

"I'm sorry, but he needs a woman," Curtis stated. "It's been so long since he came here, I honestly don't know the last time I saw his smile reach his eyes."

"I do," she answered. "It was that day at the courthouse when he had Trevor and that woman... Mara? In his arms. Since she left, even his family hasn't been able to make him smile."

"That's what happens when the love of your life leaves you," Curtis put his arm around her shoulders. "Not that I would know," he winked.

"Listen to you," she shook her head. "Did they ever work it out?"

"She's not here is she?" he asked. "So, I would assume not."

"Poor thing. Even Charlotte told me she tried to set him up with some women she works with, but he never seemed interested." Her younger daughter was turning thirty-four and married with a son of her own, but both women worried about Emmet.

"He and Mara were married," Curtis stated. "Maybe he's not able to."

"Surely not," she said. "Surely they had that annulled."

"I don't know, I haven't talked to him about it."

"What can we do?"

"Let's see if Charlotte and Derek can take Trevor home with her tonight after they get here and let's the three of us go out. Maybe to an Irish pub will help him. There's that one on Mass Ave."

"Don't you think he'll be a little Irished out?" She asked.

"Possibly," he agreed. "But if we can help him feel at home it might be better for our conversation to try and help him." Joann nodded and kissed his cheek. "Come now, let's go and look around a little. I'm going to get us another round of

Guinness and I'll meet you over there," he motioned to the large tent where several people were milling around looking at some Irish collections.

Joann agreed and headed that way, her worry for Emmet growing with every step. True, they had a rocky beginning but since he moved to America and took up being a father to Trevor, her respect and love for him grew tenfold. Losing her daughter to Ovarian Cancer when Trevor was two, broke her heart but she had her grandson to think of. When Emmet entered the picture, she was scared she would lose the last piece of her daughter she had left. However, all the stories her daughter told about him and how he took to being a father so quickly, not to mention how he moved his whole life to America so Curtis and Joann would have Trevor in their lives, Emmet had wormed his way into her heart and she loved him as a son.

His heart hurt and she couldn't help but think both she and Curtis had caused some of it. If they hadn't been so dead set on getting custody of Trevor, Emmet would have had a little more freedom and not have to prove to them he was a good father. The only way he would be get back to the carefree, fun-loving man her daughter told her about, was if Curtis and Joann loosened the invisible reigns holding him. But with that, she could lose her grandson.

As she aimlessly looked through a box filled with genealogy, her fingers stopped on one name in particular: O'Quinn.

Pulling out the paper in a protective sheath she read the meaning of the name, *wisdom.* She could use some to try and figure out what to do. But knowing it would make a good gift for Emmet, even though he probably knew all about his family name, she took it up to the register to pay.

The man behind the table smiled at her, "anything else we can help you with?" he asked, and she was a little surprised to hear an Irish accent from him. Even with Emmet in their lives, it was still unique to hear someone else from there.

"No, thank you," she smiled, and he rang up the coat of

arms. "Actually, yes..." he turned back to her. "This might be a little strange, but... do you ever miss Ireland so much it hurts?" Taking a step back, it was clear her question surprised him. "The father of my grandson is from Ireland and I can't help but wonder if he's truly happy here or if he's only here for us. I shouldn't have pried. I'm sorry."

"No, it's all right. Ireland is home for me but I've been here twenty years or so. Married an American girl. I will always miss it, but I know my life is here and I'm happy. Yes, there are times I miss Ireland and if I had a choice, I would go back. But my life is here now, and I would never leave it all behind just to go home."

"But what if you were able to take your life, all of it and go," she started. "Would you do it?"

He thought for a moment, locked eyes with her over his glasses and a sad smile ticked up the corner of his mouth. "In a heartbeat." Without another word, he wrapped the coat of arms and gave her the receipt.

She thanked him and accepted the wrapped parcel. Leaving the tent, she was so caught up in her thoughts, she didn't hear Trevor call for her until his little form rushed to her and wrapped his arms around her waist.

"Gramma! I really *really* want a wolfhound. Can you and grampa get one? Daddy says they're too big for our apartment."

She smiled down at her grandson's enthusiasm then her eyes trailed up to Emmet walking up to them.

"You know your dad knows what's best for you, honey. If he says no to the wolfhound then it's a no," she said.

"But he didn't say *you* couldn't have one," Trevor looked up at her, his arms still wrapped around her waist.

"Trev, you know your grandparents would do anything for you but getting one of those wee beasties is probably not on the top of their list," Emmet says.

"I can convince them," he grinned.

"Convince us to do what?" Curtis asked, walking up and handing Emmet another beer and a wine for his wife.

"Your grandson wants one of those," Joann motioned to one of the largest dogs Curtis had ever seen.

"Please grampa, please? I won't ask for anything ever again!"

"Today," Curtis mumbled good naturedly. Emmet chuckled and offered his hand.

"Come on, son, lets go listen to some music."

"Are Aunt Charlotte and Uncle Derek and Peter coming?" He asked as he took Emmet's hand. "Maybe I can ask them."

"They should be here any minute, sweetie," Joann replied.

Both she and Curtis watched them walk to the area of chairs in front of the stage, with a band playing an Irish ballad. They said nothing but Curtis put a hand on her shoulder and they shared a look.

CHAPTER
TWENTY-SEVEN

Emmet loved his son, he did, but if Trevor mentioned a dog one more time, he was going to have to lay some ground rules. Jacks passed away three months after Emmet was shot and though it had been years, the pain was still sharp and fresh. It was one more thing attacking him that day. First, it was *Raglan Road* and all those damned feelings about Mara and home. Then, the painful feeling of missing his family and losing his dog all over again. He wanted to give Trevor a well-rounded childhood and give him some joy since his mom died and that meant a dog to some little kids but just the thought of getting another and loving it only to lose it again was something Emmet could not do yet.

"Daddy," Trevor's voice was soft, but it pulled Emmet out of his thoughts.

"Aye?" he asked.

"Do you think my mom would have like the dogs?"

As if Emmet's heart could take anymore that day...

Trevor had asked about his mother in the past, but it had

been a while since the last time. Emmet took a deep breath.

"You know I think she would," he said. They stopped and Emmet crouched down. "Listen, son, if you are a good boy and help your grandma and granddad without complaining for two days while I'm at work, I will take you to the humane society and we will pick out a dog."

Trevor lit up. "Really?"

"Really, I promise. But you have to be good and show me you are old enough to have one."

"I promise, Daddy! I will be the best little boy you could hope for!" Trevor threw his arms around his neck.

"You already are, son," Emmet smiled and swept him up into his arms, settling him against his hip. "Now, do you know the name of the song they're playing?"

"*Red is the Rose*," Trevor replied.

"That's right, I'm impressed."

"It was one of mom's favorites. Gramma plays it sometimes when she misses her," Trevor looked down at his father's collar. "Do you miss mommy?"

"I do," he admitted. Even though their relationship lasted about as long as it takes milk to curdle, he missed her. She gave him his most precious gift and he couldn't even thank her.

"When you marry, will she be my new mommy?"

Emmet froze. "What? What are you talking about, big man?"

"I heard gramma saying to Aunt Charlotte you can't be single forever. That you're unhappy. Is it because of me you're unhappy?"

"Trevor," Emmet gasped and twisted his son around to look him the eye. "Never ever think that, understand? You make me happy. The happiest I've ever been. Never think that, all right?"

Trevor nodded. "But will you marry? Will I have a mommy again? I kinda want one, then we can be like the *Three Musketeers* you read to me."

"I don't know, Trev. I don't really think about it. But just because I may have a girlfriend doesn't mean she'll be my wife, nor your mother. It will take a special woman to fit in with us, don't you think?"

Trevor nodded. "I just don't want you sad. I watch you sometimes when you see something. It makes you sad, maybe having someone else will make you happy."

"Trevor, let's not talk about this right now, all right? You are all I need. You know that, right? I love you."

"I love you too, daddy," he threw his arms around Emmet's neck and squeezed. Pulling back, he giggled when Emmet ruffled his hair.

"Now, how about one of those funny hats you wanted?"

"Yes!" Trevor exclaimed as they walked over to the other tent.

Emmet wasn't sure what Trevor's grandparents were up to when they invited him to a local Irish pub after Charlotte and Derek agreed to take Trevor for the evening. But he was surprised. In all the years he had been in Indianapolis, he had never been there. The pub was quaint, still much larger than his local back home, but probably one of the most authentic looking pubs he had seen in America, apart from a few in Chicago he had visited when on a business trip.

As they were seated toward the front, Emmet saw a small stage near the back along with a microphone, amps, and a guitar in a stand.

"There's live music tonight," Curtis chimed happily accepting the menu.

"Yes, we are excited about this one. They're from Ireland," the hostess said.

"Oh? Emmet is from there," Curtis indicated him.

"Really? Oh, you have to talk! I just love the accent," she gushed. Emmet nodded a thanks but said nothing, pretending to look at the menu. When the twenty-one-year-old hostess left, Emmet eyed Curtis over the menu.

"What?" Curtis asked innocently.

"Don't quit your day job and become a matchmaker," Emmet replied. "Not if that's the best you got."

Curtis chuckled. "She is a little young for you."

"About a decade too young," Emmet answered. "I've done the sorority types in my time, but I'm not interested in that. Give me a little credit in discernment." He winked.

"Oh, we do, honey," Joann jumped in. "You dated our daughter after all."

"Very true," he smiled fondly. For the past four years, Emmet had gotten to know Trevor's mother more than he ever had during their vacation fling. She was an amazing mother and a wonderful woman. Part of him was sad he never truly knew her and had let a woman like that slip through his fingers. She would never have left him bleeding in the hospital. He shook his head to clear it. Every time he thought of a woman, Mara was never far from his thoughts.

The waiter came to the table and Emmet pushed back to look up at him. He was grateful it was a man with a wedding ring and didn't give Curtis a chance to try out *that* sort of a relationship for him.

When their Guinness was placed before them, they all cheered and drank. An announcement was made over the microphone that the group would be starting in a couple minutes but the way the table was set up in relation to the stage, Emmet's view was blocked by a post and a beveled glass window with a stained-glass shamrock. Joann and Curtis sat across from him on the aisle with a clear view to their left.

"Looks like it's a man and a woman but their backs are to us. I don't know if you'll know them," Curtis said leaning forward again.

Emmet chuckled. "Not everyone in Ireland knows everyone."

"True, but you might," Joann winked.

"Let me guess the woman is a redhead and you're trying to see if she's married," Emmet said.

"No, she's a brunette and it does look like she had a ring on but it's too hard to see from here."

Emmet just shook his head at Curtis's obvious interest and his blatant disregard for Emmet's *I'm not dating now* rule.

"Sláinte," he cheered to get their focus back.

"Cheers," they clinked their glasses together and settled in.

"So, what's good here?" Emmet asked.

"Everything," Curtis and Joann said together.

The waiter came back, and they ordered. They were quiet for a long moment just drinking their beer until Joann spoke up. "Emmet? Are you all right? We didn't think an Irish Festival would or could be so nostalgic for you. I'm sure you were probably homesick."

"I am," he admitted. "I know we've been there a couple times before so I'm not sure why it had such an effect on me. But I'm with Trevor and that's where I want to be and where I should be. It was just a lot today. I'll be happy to get to bed tonight. I think I'm just tired."

"You've been taking such good care of Trevor you haven't had a chance to get out with adults. We hope you don't mind us asking Charlotte and Derek to take him," Joann stated.

"Not at all," Emmet answered. "He's a wonderful kid but

I needed something other than mac and cheese or chicken nuggets. Not to mention a good beer. Thank you, both for thinking of me and inviting me out."

"We love this place, and wanted to share it with you," Joann said. "I wondered if you would be too Irished out for one day."

"Honestly this place is great and very similar to my local back home. It's nice."

"Oh good! Once we have dinner, we'll drive you back to your car and you'll have your whole apartment to yourself tonight," Joann smiled.

It happened rarely but when it happened, Emmet enjoyed his nights alone. Normally having a couple beers or a whiskey and binge watching something unfit for Trevor to see.

The waiter refilled their water glasses just as the band introduced themselves and they began to sing an Irish ballad. Curtis attempted to look but was distracted by Joann talking about Trevor's school starting up after summer break in a couple weeks.

The harmony between the man and woman did the song justice but Emmet was too focused on the topic of conversation to pay attention. However, their conversation lulled at the right moment and they heard clearly.

"Thank you all for being here tonight. We are *Celtic Spirit.* I am going to hand it off to my beautiful partner who has a real treat for you tonight," the man said.

There was a pause then, "thank you, Colm," a female voice began. "I wanted to give you a little background on this song. It is one of my absolute favorites. I recently... lost someone I cared deeply for, not to death but to something even more final, betrayal. I left him when I should have been strong and I will never know what happened to him, but I hope one day he'll hear this and think of me with kindness and maybe if I'm lucky, love."

The lights dimmed and she began acapella, the haunting

melody of *Raglan Road*. Curtis leaned back to see who it was with such a crystal-clear voice. When he saw her face, his eyes grew wide and flashed to Emmet. Emmet's white knuckled grip on his Guinness was what he saw first then Emmet met his eyes. He pleaded with him to say it was a horrible dream.

Curtis looked at his wife and her eyes reflected the same surprise and even horror. Emmet's face was pale and his hand shook. Sliding out of the booth, he had to get away. Excusing himself from the table, he did not dare look toward the stage, but he knew that voice. He knew that voice intimately and in his dreams.

Walking to the bar, he made sure to get a stool away from the eye line of the singer. Waving the bartender over, he needed a large whiskey.

"What'll have?" the bartender whispered.

"Whiskey neat, make it a large one," Emmet replied.

"Preference?"

"Irish," he answered. The barman pulled down a bottle of Jameson and poured. Placing it before him, Emmet downed it in one gulp. "Another."

Raising his brows but seeing Emmet was far from drunk, he poured another.

"Where you from?" he asked.

"Kerry, you?" Emmet replied.

"Galway, me," he answered. "How long you been here?"

"'Bout three years."

"Going on ten for me, I love it," their conversation stalled, the bartender turned back to the music as the woman finished the song and received applause and cat calls which made Emmet's hair rise on the back of his neck.

"Pretty little thing, huh?" the bartender said to the three men seated near Emmet. "Too bad she's married." Emmet's eyes shot up. "What do you reckon, the man?"

"Probably that," one of the guests said. "Pity. But if you see that rock. She's done well."

Emmet tossed back the whiskey and looked away. Slamming down the glass, he ordered another. Curtis walked up and leaned against the bar. He said nothing but Emmet felt his eyes on him.

"What?" he demanded a little too harshly. Curtis shrugged his shoulders. "Did Joann ask you to check up on me?"

"Yes, but I was already on my way over to you."

"I'm fine."

"Bull shit," Curtis said. "What happened between you two?"

"She ended it, just like she said."

"Have you tried to talk to her?"

"Yeah, I did in the hospital when she walked out of my life forever."

"Did she tell you why?" Curtis asked.

"It doesn't matter."

"You still care for her, I can see it."

"No, I don't," Emmet tossed back another whiskey. Finally, some of the pain was easing from his chest with the cloudiness of his mind.

"Don't kid a kidder, son. You haven't gotten over her."

"It doesn't matter. Apparently, she's married... again."

"When was the last time you were with a woman?" Curtis asked.

"What? None of your damn business that's when," Emmet replied heatedly. The men around him were doing a terrible job of pretending not to listen. "Besides, I'm a father now."

"Doesn't mean you stopped being human. And a man,"

Curtis said. "And what does being a father have to do with it?"

"It's not like I can bring a woman home with my son sleeping in the other room."

"True, but you know you have us, we can always watch him for you if that were to happen," Curtis said. "Now's your chance. Go talk to her. Figure out what happened."

"I know what happened. Her crazy ex put two bullets in my chest and she left me. End of story."

"Wrong, not end of story and you have a chance to find out the end now."

Emmet huffed a sigh. "I'm going for a walk." Pulling out his wallet, he set a few bills on the counter and left.

CHAPTER
TWENTY-EIGHT

The walk did little to clear his mind, but it helped with the stuffiness of the bar. He would have stayed out later, but his stomach rumbled, and he remembered he hadn't had a single bite of his hamburger nor any lunch. Rounding the bend in the street, he saw a man and a woman leaning against the wall, sharing a cigarette. He paid them no attention as he skirted past but the moment he did, he heard a gasp from the woman.

"Emmet?" He stopped and turned slowly to see her standing in the shadows. "Is it really you? Oh my god!"

"Mara," he spat out the name as quickly as he could, like ripping off a band aid.

"Oh my god, it is you!" She rushed toward him, but he took a step back and put out his hand to stop her. She looked at him, then down. "Are you all right? It's been years. I'm so sorry. I had to leave. As soon as Ben was behind bars, I tried to find you, but you had left, and no one would tell me where you were. I figured you came to the States, but I didn't know where. I'm so glad you're here. It's so good to see you."

"I wish I could say the same, good evening," he turned and took two steps.

"Wait!" she cried. "Please, wait. I... I was trying to protect you and your son. I always loved you!"

"Really?" He turned to face her. "Then you leaving me in the hospital was your way of showing it? If I remember correctly, your exact words were *I never loved you.*"

"My god..." she gasped. "You hate me."

"No Mara, I loved you, and god help me, I still do but what you did... I can never forgive."

"I did what I did to protect you."

"You left me when I needed you most," he tried to keep his voice down but failed. Taking a step back, he thrust his hands through his hair. "I'm sorry, I didn't mean to yell but, dammit, do you have any idea what you put me through?"

"Yes, I do, because I put myself through the same."

"Mar, we need to go," her friend said.

"Just give me a second," she called back.

"Go. You need to finish your set," Emmet said.

"You were in there?"

"I see the talent scout worked out then."

She looked at the back the door then to Emmet again. "Please, we need to talk but I have to finish my set. I'm staying at the Hilton Gardens. Please meet me for coffee. There's a place just around the corner from the hotel. Please, Em. Nine-thirty? Please." He paused.

"Mara, we have to go," her friend called again.

"Please, Emmet," she begged.

"Shouldn't you ask your husband before asking your ex husband out for coffee?" Emmet asked, indicating the other singer by the door.

"What?" she questioned.

"I hear from the men at the bar congratulations are in order," Emmet replied. "Looks like you did well for yourself. I hope he knows what he has in you."

"Emmet," she paused, then raised her left hand for him to see. "I'm not married to anyone but you. Never have been."

Emmet stared at the ring on her finger. It was the one he purchased for her in the antique store in Sligo Town.

"Please meet me at the coffee shop. Please."

He nodded dumbly, his mouth and throat completely dry. "Okay," he croaked. "Maybe." He corrected.

She sighed in relief and raced to the back door the man was holding open for her. With a glance back at Emmet, she smiled, and he felt something loosen within him.

But one thing was certain, he could not listen to the rest of her singing. Hurrying back into the pub, Emmet found Curtis and Joann still sitting at their table, their meals done and a to-go box at his place.

"Emmet, are you all right? I wanted Curtis to go look for you, but he refused. Said you needed to be on your own," Joann said.

"We're all settled up here and at the bar. We can leave whenever," Curtis offered.

"I'm fine, Joann, thank you. Thanks for settling up for me. I'd like to head out now," Emmet replied.

They gathered their things and Emmet grabbed his to-go box, without looking at Mara whose gaze he could feel on his back. He left the restaurant as Colm started strumming strains of *She Moved Thru' the Fair* on his guitar.

Seeing Emmet leave the restaurant was harder than

Mara thought it would be. But she would recognize his frame anywhere and when she saw him push open the door without turning back to look at her, her thoughts immediately went to the coffee meeting, she all but begged him to attend. If he would show, she didn't know. But the little spark of hope at seeing him again, she had kept alive for four years was starting to fan into a larger flame. It could cause trouble if he wasn't interested in her any longer. There was also a little something she had never told him about regarding their marriage license. She held out hope he would come around. Hoping and praying their serendipitous moment of meeting at an Irish pub in Indianapolis, of all places, wasn't merely a fluke and Fate was smiling down at her. They finished their set at midnight, had a quick round with the manager, collected their earnings and soon she and Colm were on their way to the hotel.

Sleep elusive, she scrolled through the photos she had on her phone of Emmet at his parent's cottage. Stopping on one in particular, she caressed the photo of him sleeping. Their night together was well engrained in her mind. She remembered his tender kisses, fiery touches and sweet caresses. She had taken the photo when he fell asleep. Always loving how peaceful he looked while asleep, it wasn't the first time she stared at the picture.

Her eyes were heavy. Setting the phone on her pillow, she snuggled deeper into the bed and staring at his sleeping face. Even a photo made her remember how safe she felt in his arms, how loved and how she completely ruined it for them both.

Chapter
Twenty-Nine

The next morning Mara got up, showered and dressed with surprising energy after having only slept a couple hours. It was one of the longest nights of her life apart from the night Emmet was in surgery four years ago. As she stared at her reflection in the hotel bathroom mirror, she tried to calm her shaking hands. It was only nine in the morning but if she stayed in the hotel room any longer, she was going to go stir crazy. One last look at her reflection and she grabbed her purse and headed out the door. Walking slowly to the elevator then down the street when she left, she tried to will time to go faster. Finally, the coffee place was in sight.

With a final deep breath, she pushed open the door. It was busy for a Sunday morning, but she got in line and waited for her turn. She nearly laughed at the name of the special coffee. In the honor of the Irish Festival in town, they had a coffee named *The Nutty Irishman*.

Meeting her own nutty Irishman, she had to get one. Sitting in one of the two comfortable chairs in the corner by the windows, she checked her phone. Nine thirty-five. Emmet wasn't there. When nine forty rolled around, her heart was heavy, and her stomach fell. He wasn't coming. The line had diminished as had her coffee. She stood and went to the barista. Once she got her second cup, she turned to leave and nearly ran into the man behind her. Catching her cup before she spilled it on his blue polo, "sorry," she said and looked up. Seeing Emmet standing there, her heart kicked into overdrive and her knees went weak. "Emmet," she breathed.

"I'm sorry I'm late," he said.

"No," she shook her head. "That's okay. I'm glad you're here. I have a place by the window, unless you'd like to sit outside?"

"Window is fine," he replied.

"Okay, they have good coffee here," she gestured to her cup.

Emmet looked at her and only then did she realize she stood in his way. Stepping away, she went back to her chair and waited, her eyes zeroed onto his back. He had changed, filled out a little more. He wasn't as defined as he was before, but Mara preferred him that way. She found herself jealous of the barista simply because he was able to carry on a conversation with Emmet and get him to smile. What she wouldn't give to bask in the warmth of Emmet's smile once more. Finally, he got his coffee and headed over to her, his steps slow and measured, cautious.

When he reached her, he sat down in the open seat beside her and held his cup, picking at the cardboard warmer sleeve.

"Thank you for coming," she finally said.

He nodded and took a sip. "I almost didn't."

"I figured," she answered looking away. "I'm glad you did, though."

They were quiet for a moment then both turned to each

other and said their names at the same time as if starting a conversation, then they paused again.

"Go ahead," Emmet offered.

"Emmet, I'm sorry."

"You said that last night," he replied.

"Well I am. When I left you…"

"In the hospital, with two holes in my chest…" he completed. She bit back the tears but nodded.

"It was to protect you. They had caught him, and I wanted to make sure he was put away before he could hurt anyone else. Especially you and Trevor. The trial and sentencing took a whole year and when he was finally put away, I looked for you, but you were gone. I begged your family, Tom, and Chloe to tell me where you were, but they wouldn't. I wanted to make sure you were okay."

"I wasn't," he said. She looked at him for a long moment before he decided to continue. "When you left, I was wrecked. I loved you so much and life had just begun for us. I had my son and you. Then you left, not only left but told me you never loved me. My wife. The woman I wanted to build a life with. The woman I wanted to raise my son with. It was clear you did not want to be with me." She began to protest but he raised a hand stopping her. "Please, I let you talk." She nodded and looked down. "I tried to call you, text you, go see you but you did not want to see me. I hoped what you said was only temporary because of Ben's arrest but after months of nothing from you I realized you had to have meant it. Ness told me when you came by asking about me. She wanted to tell you, but I told her no. And now, here you are, still wearing my ring?"

"I wanted to tell you. I wanted to find you and tell you how much I love you. It was only to keep you and Trevor safe but when no one would tell me and my singing career took off, I hoped I would be able to travel the world and maybe one day find you. I want to pick up where we left off."

"How do you know I haven't moved on?" he asked.

She felt the blood drain from her face. She had to tell him but didn't know how. "I don't know... All I know is I love you."

"I love you too," he conceded. "But no. I can't. I can't do that to me, to Trevor. I will always, god help me, love you, but Mara... no."

"Why?" she squeaked out.

"Because I cannot open that door. I'm sorry. The story of our love is over."

"I refuse to think that."

"Then you're in for a disappointment, I'm sorry," he stood to leave. "I will never regret our time together but I'm not the same man you left in that hospital. I'm sorry."

"Emmet, wait, please," she rushed after him, following him out the door and onto the sidewalk. He stopped and turned to her.

"Mara, stop, it's over," Emmet stated.

"No, please," she grabbed his shirt and pulled him to her. Without thinking, she pressed her lips to his. He tried to pull away at first, but she felt his desperation as if it was her own and the second his resistance broke. He gave in to her kiss and kissed her back.

When they finally pulled away, she said nothing about the hungry look in his eyes, only took his hand and pulled him toward the hotel.

They still said nothing as they waited for the elevator, nor when they had to share with three others and the floors were lower than Mara's. The only outward sign of nerves she saw was Emmet tapping his index finger on his thigh.

Finally, they were alone in the elevator. Mara half expected Emmet to grab her and push her against the wall, kissing her like in a movie she had seen, but he didn't. He simply waited. Once the elevator dinged at her eighth floor, she was nearly crazy with anticipation. Emmet followed her down the hall to her room. She slid the key card into the lock and opened the door. She took three steps into the room and closed her eyes when she heard the door close and latch, unsure if Emmet had taken the steps behind her.

When his hands came softly on her upper arms, she gasped and leaned back against his chest. He moved her hair away from her right shoulder. She followed the movement with her head giving him better access to her neck. Her Irishman did not disappoint. His lips tenderly caressed her skin sending goosebumps all over her arms and down her legs.

"Emmet," she breathed as his teeth grazed the pounding tendon in her neck. She turned around and looked up into his blue eyes, sliding her hands up his arms to latch together behind his neck. They held each other's gazes and slowly, he lowered his lips to hers. She never broke their connection except when he pulled her shirt over her head. Her hands found his belt and she pulled it off just as quickly. His shirt followed and soon they stood together, their lips never stopped moving.

With gentle but firm command, Emmet backed her to the bed. When the back of her knees hit the mattress, she sank down, loving the heat and pressure of Emmet's bare chest on hers as he followed her down.

"I love you," she moaned. He didn't say it back, but she felt it in every caress, every kiss and every move.

CHAPTER
THIRTY

Emmet lay on his back, Mara's body snug against his side, her head resting on his shoulder and her fingers toying with the hair on his chest. When she rose on her elbow, she slowly lowered her lips to the bullet scar on his sternum and the other just below his left pectoral. She locked eyes with him but said nothing. His hand buried in the thick mass of her brunette hair and he pulled her down to rest her head on the middle of his chest.

When Curtis had asked at the bar, how long it had been for him, he did not want to admit the last time he had slept with a woman had been that all-too-short time with Mara four years ago. No other woman had come close to her, let alone, he had made vows before God to that woman and he wasn't about to break them.

He had dates to humor Charlotte's desires to set him up with someone, but they always ended the same way; stale, a kiss on the cheek goodnight and a text later in the week that said she didn't feel a spark with him and was sorry, but they could always be friends. Not that he felt comfortable even being at the pool shirtless, let alone intimate with anyone. After being shot, his usual gym routine was out of the question. Packing on about fifty to seventy-five pounds and losing his movie star physique, didn't add to his confidence level. But with Mara, he didn't feel any of that. It was almost like with her, his body, his looks, his age didn't matter. He didn't realize until that moment how lonely he was.

Yes, he had his son, but not a connection with a woman like he felt with Mara. He was about to say how much he missed her, when she moved, looked up at him and sighed. "I wish I didn't have to leave tonight."

And just like that, his walls went back up and he closed himself off. "You're leaving?" he stated. Somehow, he wasn't surprised.

The look in her eyes showed she heard the tightness in his voice and felt the tension in his body. She looked away.

"Colm and I are playing a gig tonight at the Irish Fest and then we need to be in Chicago by Tuesday. Our manager likes us to leave directly after the show, so we have time to rest up before the next one."

Emmet didn't know what to say. Logically, he knew that was a rational reason but all he could feel was the pain of his stitches ripping as he tried to go after her at the hospital four years ago.

"We go to the park ahead of today's event at two," she went on. "We play for an hour and fifteen minutes at three-fifteen. We're the last gig of the night. We played Friday too, it was great exposure. I think we're going to a restaurant downtown afterward."

"It's past noon," Emmet started, looking at the clock. "You should probably get ready. I'll head out."

"Please, don't," she said.

"I have to," those words tasted bitter as he remembered

when she had said the same to him. "Good luck today. I'm glad your dream came true." Swinging his legs over the side of the bed, he sat up and pulled on his clothes. Standing, he did not look back at her as he grabbed his polo off the floor.

"My tour is almost over," she began. "Come back with me, Emmet. Come home."

He closed his eyes at the immediate ache in his chest. He hadn't been back to Ireland in four years. It would be wonderful to go back and see his home and his family. He hadn't seen his dad and stepmom in all four years. It would also be good to see how little Cait and Liam were doing, since they had grown so much since he'd been away.

He missed his family something fierce but for his own sanity, he had to keep away. He Skyped with them nearly every week but there was nothing like receiving one of his father's hugs and picking his stepmother up in a big bear hug, followed by one of her loving reproaches, usually with a wooden spoon in her hand, striking his shoulder. Or having a true homecooked meal with some of his ma's specialties. He missed them and home, but Mara was everywhere in Ireland and he couldn't bear to go back, even after what just happened between them. He couldn't open that door. If that made him a coward, so be it.

He couldn't uproot his son nor take him away from his grandparents. Curtis and Joann had been godsends watching Trevor while he was at work. Of course, a six-year-old was much easier to handle than a one or two year old but he wouldn't repay their kindness by taking him away.

"I can't," he said. "You have no idea how much I want to. But my life is in America. I miss Ireland. I miss my family, but no. For my son's sake, I cannot."

She said nothing as he pulled on his shoes and when he went to the door, he half expected her to call him back. But when all she said was a soft; "goodbye, Emmet," he stopped and turned, taking one more look at her face. She didn't cry. She didn't beg. She merely held his gaze, telling him everything he ever needed to hear in that one look.

"Goodbye, Mara," he stated, then without another word, opened the door and walked down the hall to the elevator.

The drive to pick Trevor up from his aunt's and uncle's was one of the longest Emmet had ever experienced and they were only a stone's throw from downtown.

Could he actually be considering uprooting everything Trevor knew merely to satisfy the longing in his heart for home and the need for Mara? How selfish could he be? Seeing her again, kissing her again, making love to her, it turned his nice, neat little world, topsy-turvy.

Pulling into Charlotte's driveway, he waited in the car for a minute. He still loved her, that much was clear. Could he ask her to make a go of it but in America? She obviously travelled a lot. Maybe he could travel with her some of the time and he and Trevor could go back to Ireland for her concerts there. How would his job handle him being gone for any long length of time? One thing he learned quickly in America was, the jobs do not let you take time off. They may say they do but if you try to take time, it's heavily frowned upon and could cost you a promotion. He couldn't afford to lose his job, not only were they friends of Curtis, but they had added to his visa application and helped him get to America. Any way he tried to slice it, he was stuck.

The front door of the house opened, and Trevor stood behind the glass storm-door waving and smiling wildly. Just seeing his little boy, he knew he could never do what Mara asked. His place was with that crazy, amazing, wonderful little boy. Popping the door open, he stepped out of the car and braced for his son to run and jump into his arms. Trevor didn't disappoint.

"Daddy!" Trevor exclaimed excitedly as he jumped and threw his arms around Emmet's neck giving him a big hug.

"How's my big man?" Emmet asked, hugging him.

"Good," he said then pulled back to look at him. "You *have* to see what Aunt Charlotte and Uncle Derek and Peter and me did!"

"Peter and I," Emmet lovingly corrected.

"Peter and I," Trevor learned. "We made pizza!"

"Pizza, huh?" Emmet asked as he saw Charlotte at the door. Heading over, he greeted her. "I hope he was good for you."

"The best," Charlotte answered reciprocating his one-armed hug and kiss on the cheek. She looked at him sheepishly, when he pulled back. His confused gaze followed her fingers as she touched a place on her own neck and raised her brows. Unfortunately, Trevor was too quick and observant.

"Daddy, why do you have a red mark on your neck? Did you hurt yourself?"

Shite, he thought. He had a hickey. "I must have scratched myself, lad. I'm all right. Show me those pizzas."

Trevor squirmed out of his arms and he set him down before he was dragged by his hand to the kitchen. Thankfully, Charlotte said nothing about the mark. He would need to ask for some makeup to cover it up and he would need to make sure he did not take off his shirt for a couple days. He remembered Mara's nails raking down his back and he was sure he bore the marks.

After they showed the pizzas still in the oven, Emmet asked Charlotte into the study while Trevor and Peter played with Charlotte's husband Derek in the living room.

"Do you have some concealer?" he asked. Her playful eyes reminded him of Ness back home.

She motioned for him to follow her down the hall and to the master bath. As she dug in her makeup kit, she caught his eyes briefly in the mirror.

"Who is she?" she asked.

"What do you mean?" he replied.

"The woman who gave you that hickey," she clarified. "I'm guessing it's a woman," she winked.

Emmet huffed a sigh. *Yep, just like Ness.*

"It's someone I knew… back in Ireland," he admitted.

She turned with a tube of liquid slightly darker than his skin tone.

"Are you going to see her again?" She asked. He held out his hand for the tube of concealer.

"Since when are you this interested in my sex life?" Emmet teased.

"Since all my single friends gave up on you," she cracked.

He breathed a laugh but sighed. "I have and always will be thankful to you for setting me up on those blind dates but, Char, I just can't see anyone right now."

"So, you're going to steal away and have Sunday morning quickies until… when? Trevor's eighteen?"

"If I have to," he replied.

"Look," she sighed. "You're like a brother to me. I'm under no delusion my sister loved you or you her, but you are the father of her only child. And she always talked about you with fondness. Emmet, you can't hold yourself to such extremes. You're a man and you are a damn good father. It's time you live a little."

"Her life is on the road and in Ireland. I couldn't put Trevor through that."

"Interesting," she began.

"What?"

"I said live a little and you immediately thought of a life with her." Emmet crossed his arms over his chest. "Food for thought. Now let me apply this so you don't have to come up with another excuse for a hickey to Trevor."

Emmet stood still and allowed Charlotte to apply the

make up on his neck, his mind far too confused to respond. Fortunately, Charlotte stayed quiet and as soon as she finished, they went to the main room and enjoyed the pizzas. Mara was never far from his thoughts nor Charlotte's advice.

CHAPTER THIRTY-ONE

Trevor was asleep by the time they pulled into the parking spot at their apartment. Unbuckling him from the car booster seat, Emmet grabbed his little overnight backpack and carried his son up the walk to their door. Fishing the keys out of his pocket, Emmet opened the door and let them in.

Trevor didn't wake for longer than it took to get him into his superhero pjs and brush his teeth. Emmet didn't even need to read him a bedtime story. As soon as his head hit the pillow, he was out. Kissing his son's forehead, he turned on his little leprechaun nightlight and snuck out of his room.

Pouring himself a small glass of whiskey, he sat on the couch and turned on the TV. Alone as usual, a sense of emptiness filled him as he looked beside him to the vacant spot on the sofa. For a moment, he saw Mara's form and smiling face beside him, but it was gone as quickly as it was there.

She had hit thirty-two last October and was approaching forty in a year, but she looked damned good and soon he caught himself fantasizing about her. Forcing his mind to another topic, any topic, he faced the TV only to see one of his favorite celebrity chefs having a heart to heart with a restaurant owner about how he had a good woman within his grasp, and he was an idiot if he let her go. Well, that didn't help. His phone buzzed on the sofa next to him and he sighed when he saw who it was.

"Evening, Curtis," he answered.

"Emmet, how are you?" Curtis asked.

"I'm fine, and you and Joann?"

"We're doing well, yeah just – uh – thought I'd give you a call and see how things are going."

"Charlotte called Joann, didn't she?" Emmet asked.

"Uh – well – um – why – why would you ask that?"

"Look," he sighed. "Everything is fine. I appreciate her looking after Trevor for a little longer than expected this morning. But it won't happen again."

"We just wanted to let you know, it's okay if it does, sweetie," Joann's voice came from the speaker. They must be gathered around Curtis' phone.

"Well, I appreciate that but it's not going to happen again."

"Emmet, it's time you live a little," Curtis stated. "And if Mara is in town, it's high time you two made up and consider settling down. You don't have to prove anything to us, we know you're a damn fine father."

"It doesn't matter, she's leaving tonight anyway. Her life is on the road. She wouldn't settle just to be with me. And I wouldn't want her to. She's an amazing singer, that's her passion. And besides, she's based out of Ireland. I couldn't go nor could I take Trevor away from you. It wouldn't be right to uproot him. He's happy here."

"But you're not," Joann said softly.

"I'm a parent, Joann, you know how it is. My happiness

is my son's happiness."

"Would you go back? If there were no obstacles? Would you go home?" she asked.

"There are obstacles so I don't think it would be best to speculate," Emmet stated.

"Do you love her?" Joann asked.

"I—" it was on the tip of Emmet's tongue to say no simply because it would be the easiest thing to do, but it felt like a disservice. He heaved a sigh. "Yes, I do."

"And does she love you?"

"Yes, she does," he answered.

"Then you need to fight for it," Joann stated. "I already lost one of my children, I won't lose another."

It took a moment for Emmet to understand what she was saying. Joann loved him like a son.

"But you would, and you would lose Trevor if I left. I couldn't be without him."

"And we would never ask that of you," Curtis interjected. "But son, we're retired. We can travel and there's so much we want to do. Yes, we would miss him, badly but what would be worse is knowing you gave up your dreams and your happiness for us. We love you and Trevor more than anything but if this is your dream, if it would make you happy, go for it. Go after her. Forgive her and be with her."

"Trevor would love living in Ireland and make no mistake, we would be there very often, so you better get a big enough place for us to stay," Joann continued.

For the first time in four years, Emmet's heart lifted and finally felt full. He still owned his old dealership and it was still there, waiting for him. Paddy and Tom worked as partners. He had plenty in his savings even after a large move three and a half years ago. He had sold his motorcycle and his car in Ireland. His job in the States was enough to let them live comfortably and replenish his savings. He would be able to support them, and his family would help him with Trevor while he started up at the dealership again. Hell, maybe his brother could enroll him in the local school and teach him. It would help Trevor's adjustment if he had a familiar face. Bloody hell, was he actually thinking about doing this? His heart screamed yes and for once, his mind stopped saying no.

"But she's leaving tonight. I won't see her again. I don't have her number either," Emmet said. "Not to mention Trevor's asleep."

"I'm on my way to watch him," Curtis said. "You get prepared so you can go after her. Do you know where she is?"

"She said she was playing this evening at the Irish Fest then they were going to have dinner in town and leave," Emmet grabbed his shoes. Curtis and Joann were only ten minutes away, a perk he never truly appreciated until that moment. "Even then, she's going to Chicago, she's on tour. I—"

"Go, you haven't had a vacation. Go with her and call us from the road. We'll take care of Trevor," Joann promised.

"I can't. I haven't told my boss. I can't just leave."

"Sure you can, call in sick Monday or I can call and let them know you had a family emergency," Curtis offered.

"But I don't know if they've left yet," Emmet replied.

"I found the band's Facebook page," Charlotte's voice chimed in.

"Char?" Emmet looked at his phone then put it to his ear. "How long have you been on the line?"

"Mom called me first and then we conferenced you in," she explained. "And what's this about you being *married* to this woman?"

"Long story," Emmet said.

"Well, I expect some answers later but," Charlotte went on. "The band guy posted a picture of their pizza and checked in.

Thanks for such a great welcome Indy. Here's to many more times," she read. "Looks like they're at Bazbeaux on Mass. That post was forty-five minutes ago. You better hurry."

"I—" he started.

"Stop with the excuses," Charlotte interrupted.

Emmet sighed harshly. "Joann, do you think you could call the restaurant and see if they are still there? Make some excuse?"

"I gotcha, honey," she said. "The man's name was?"

"Colm," he replied. "Promise me, you'll tell Trevor I love him and if I don't get home and actually do go with her to Chicago that I'm sorry I didn't tell him bye. I'll call when he's up."

"Don't worry, sweetie, Trevor will be excited. We'll tell him you're going on an adventure. He'll love it," Joann replied.

"I'm pulling in now, son," Curtis said over the conference call. "I'll be at your door in thirty seconds."

"Let yourself in," Emmet offered rushing to his closet and grabbing an extra pair of jeans, clean socks, underwear, and a couple shirts. Peeking into Trevor's room, he tiptoed to his son's bed and gazed into his sleeping face. Gently kissing his forehead, he whispered he loved him just as he heard the front door open and Curtis coming up the steps. He pulled Emmet into a backslapping hug.

"Go get your lass," he teased. "Have fun."

"Keep us connected," Charlotte called.

"But put us on mute if you want," Joann offered.

"No mom, I want to hear," Charlotte complained.

"Hush, honey, his private life is just that, private."

"The bed has clean sheets," Emmet ignored the conversation over the phone and spoke to Curtis. "Um, you're welcome to any of the food and drinks in the fridge or the bar."

"Yeah yeah, go," Curtis urged and nearly pushed Emmet

toward the stairs. Slinging the pack on his back, he took one more look at Curtis and headed out the door.

Chapter

Thirty-Two

After a weird call at the restaurant that pulled Colm away from the table for about twenty minutes, they all three piled into their manager's car and headed back to the event RV still on site at the park. It was eerie to see all the empty white tents decorating the open green. No one was around apart from some of the maintenance crew still cleaning up and a couple police officers patrolling the area.

Colm sat in the front seat of the car, giving Mara the entire backseat. Seeing, talking and sleeping with Emmet that day had worn her nerves thin. Mustering all she could for the fans, she gave a good performance with only Colm knowing something was up. He promptly asked her what was bothering her as soon as they left the stage that evening. Having been married for two years, she knew he would understand. Being a good friend, her best friend recently, she told him everything that happened both four years ago, the night before and that morning.

He was surprisingly comforting, but she could tell he

worried about the band and how this could affect them. But she had seen he and his wife make it work even if he didn't set foot on Irish soil for more than three months at a time. She joined him on the road for some of the time, but they also didn't have any children yet. It could never work for Emmet, not with Trevor, and she would never ask him to choose her over him. No, her time with Emmet was over and done, as witnessed that afternoon where she said goodbye. She would have to move on, and she would have to file divorce papers, god help her figure out how to do that. Since they were married in the courthouse, the papers were filed immediately and there was nothing she could do after they had been processed. Technically, they were still married.

The car came to a stop just beside their bus and the manager got out to start hooking the car up to the back of the bus. Colm turned in his seat to look at her. His kind blue eyes reminded her of Emmet's, when he wasn't looking at her like she had just ripped his heart out.

"You okay?" he asked. She nodded but hoped the tears that stung the back of her eyes wouldn't fall until she was safely in her bed. She could pull the curtain and let them out silently. "It'll be okay. Trust me."

She smiled at him but didn't know how any of it would be okay. "What was that call you got at dinner?" she asked, needing to change the subject before her emotions got the better of her.

He shrugged. "Some fan saw my post on Facebook and called the restaurant to tell us how much they enjoyed our concert."

"Stalkerish," she replied.

"Part of the job, sweetheart," he winked. "It felt wrong not to let her expound and tell us how great we are."

"Twenty minutes?" she asked. "Must have been a super fan."

"I also went to the restroom, so there's that," he

admitted with a funny look on his face. Mara laughed but the emotions of the day threatened to overcome her and turn her laugh into an hysterical wail. Instead, she took a deep breath, suppressing the pain. Getting out of the car, she just stared at the door of the RV. If she stepped into that bus, the history with Emmet, her husband, would be just that. History. But no matter, how many times she said or thought it, it never would ease the pain and guilt of leaving him so many years ago. Still, she had a job to do and she wasn't going to get any sleep that night by staying in the backseat. She met Colm around the side of the car and he wrapped his arm around her shoulders in a brotherly embrace. Then lowered his arm as they got to the door. She looked at Colm who smiled but she waited, unable to bring herself to open that door. Finally, she reached for the handle but Colm stopped her.

"Hey, before you do that, I think you might have a visitor," he said. She looked at him confused, then followed his gaze behind her. The figure of a man was walking over to them. In the dark, she couldn't make out his face, but she would know him anywhere.

"Emmet?" she breathed. He finally stepped into the light of the security lamp above them and she saw it was indeed him. He stared at her for a long moment, then finally spoke softly.

"I can't let you go," he began. "I tried, I did, for four years. I wanted so badly to get you out of my head and my heart but nothing I did could stop how much I love you, Mara. I'm sorry for all this time we lost, and I am so very sorry for walking away like I did this afternoon. I thought I would never be able to have the two things I wanted most in this world together. You and my son.... I thought I would always have to choose between you but that is not the case and I was a fool for thinking it. I do not have to choose, my family showed me that. It almost seemed too good to be true, but then they made me see sense and I will forever be grateful to them for that, and Colm for delaying you."

She looked over at her partner beside her. He grinned and shrugged. "His son's grandmother called the restaurant and asked for my help. After everything you told me, I figured you both needed this."

He smiled fondly at her but stepped around the bus to help their manager. Emmet took a step closer to her.

"Ever since I first held you in my arms when you were nine after you broke your ankle, I loved you. I just didn't realize it. Then when I held you again as you cried to me many years later, I knew what I wanted. I wanted to be the only one who will dry your tears and never cause them, be the only one to hold you every night, make love to you every morning, laugh with you, celebrate with you and raise my son with you. So, I guess my question to you is... is there room for one more on that bus of yours? Because I would very much like to be with you."

"What about Trevor?" she asked and only then realized tears were streaming down her cheeks.

"His grandparents and aunt and uncle are taking care of him for now but as soon as we can, we're moving back home. Ireland is still your home, right? Maybe we can make a home together... if you'll have me."

Mara couldn't speak as her throat tightened with emotion. "Have you?" she squeaked. Nodding emphatically, she wiped her tears. "Aye, my Irishman. I'll have you, gladly. And I want to be there for your son, if you'll let me. I love you Emmet."

Emmet breathed out as his tears fell. They raced to each other and he picked her up, twirling her around. He kissed her slowly, thoroughly, tasting both of their tears mixing together.

"I love you," he said again as he set her down slowly, bracing her against him.

"I love you," she replied, then gently touching the collar of his polo, she took a deep breath. "I should tell you something."

"What is it?"

"You remember when I said I petitioned the courts to annul our marriage?"

"Aye," he answered. "Though it's not a memory I want to

hold on to."

"I know. But, they couldn't. They said since we were married at the courthouse, the document was actually already filed and there was nothing they could do."

It took him a moment, but finally, a slow grin spread across his lips. "We're still married?"

"We're still married," she confirmed. "And I would very much like to stay that way... if you want."

"If I want?" Emmet barked a laugh. "I never wanted anything else!" he picked her up and twirled her around, kissing her again as she giggled.

"Looks like you'll be travelling with us for a while," Colm's voice came from the front of the RV.

"Aye, looks that way. Thank you for your help," Emmet said.

"No worries," Colm answered. "But I do have one ground rule."

"What's that?" Emmet asked.

"No sex while I'm in the caravan."

Emmet laughed as Mara blushed deeply. Thrusting his hand out to Colm, Emmet grinned broadly.

"It'll be tough, but it's a deal," he teased.

Colm took his hand and they shook on it.

"Are we all set?" their manager asked.

"Aye, we're one heavy," Colm called back.

Emmet looked at Mara as Colm again disappeared around the front of the RV. He kissed her temple then grabbed his phone out of his back pocket, took it off mute and put it on speaker. Mara saw the time duration of the call, nearly an hour. She looked over at him, but he just smiled.

"Hey everyone," he spoke into the phone. "I'm going to

Chicago."

The cheers on the other end were deafening as he received congratulations from everyone. "With my wife..." Emmet finished.

"You didn't!" an older woman's voice called.

"Looks like Mara never did get the marriage annulled. We've been married for four years, but you'll all be there when we renew our vows," Emmet revealed.

Mara looked over at him and reveled in the feeling of her Irishman holding her and as he signed off, promising to call later.

At his beckoning, she turned toward the door where Colm and her manager had already entered the RV. She went up the steps but stopped and turned to see him standing behind her. She took a second to pull out a necklace she was wearing, the long chain hiding the item beneath her shirt. Pulling it over her head, she slid the piece off the chain and extended her other hand asking to take his.

Instinctually, Emmet gave his right hand, she gently pushed it away, shook her head and looked pointedly at the left. His brows furrowed for a second, but he offered his left hand and watched as she slid a man's silver wedding ring on his finger.

"I saved this after having bought it on impulse when I found out our marriage was still valid. If you don't like it, we can get another," she said.

Emmet looked down at the ring on his finger, the Celtic engravings known as the *Celtic Warrior,* marked the silver band. It fit his finger perfectly, though it felt foreign, it felt right.

"I found it in the window of a shop in Killarney and thought of you instantly and wanted so badly to see it on your finger. I've worn it everyday except this morning because I didn't want you to see it until I knew. Do you like it?"

"Like it?" Emmet breathed. "Mara, it's perfect."

She bit her lower lip, but her grin was perpetually on her face. When they locked eyes again, his gaze promised all sorts of wonderfully wicked things just as they did when he followed her up the lane to his parent's cottage in Sligo.

This time, as with the first time, she thanked Fate to have met him again and to be given a second chance with him. Everything with Ben, Chloe, Tom, Ben's trial, everything had led them to that moment. As she took a seat on the sofa built into the side of the RV, she leaned into Emmet as he wrapped his arm around her and accepted the flute of customary celebratory champagne from Colm. After she toasted Colm to a job well done at the concert, she turned to Emmet and toasted to the rest of their lives then followed the champagne with a promising kiss. He winked and tapped his wedding ring against the glass absentmindedly. Pulling her into him, she breathed him in and snuggled while he struck up a conversation with Colm. As their manager pulled out of the parking space and got on the road for their next adventure, she thanked her lucky stars she was forced to go across the Irish Sea and find her Irishman.

an deireadh

Acknowledgements

Thank you all for reading! It has been a rollercoaster ride with Emmet O'Quinn! He has definitely been a difficult character but one of my favorites. Authors say their characters "speak to" them and it is very true. Emmet and I had an "argument" about his future and it took a very long time for us to come to an understanding. It might sound odd but it's true. He told me one thing and I refused to let my readers down by not granting him his happy ending. Fortunately, he and I came to an understanding and this is the result. It was years in the making but I think it was worth it. Emmet and Mara were a pleasure to write and I am very proud of their story.

I want to thank all my fans and those who love Emmet for sticking with me throughout these years. I hope the next novel which is Emmet's cousin Keera's story will not take as long. And actually, Trevor has started to speak with me about his story. Sixteen years later and the young, sweet six-year-old boy from this story is no longer a boy and is his father's son. I am very excited about the possibility of writing his story.

I want to thank my parents for always being supportive and understanding when I am unavailable for dinners, movie night, and weekends due to writing. They are the most amazing parents and I couldn't wish for better!

I hope you love the second installment of the *Love*

Among the Shamrocks Collection and please read on for a sneak peek at the third; *On the River Shannon*, Keera's story.

Please visit my website for more books and information! www.mkatherineclark.net.

love among the shamrocks collection

Book Three

On the

River Shannon

M. KATHERINE CLARK

1

Prologue

"Keera!" Nessa Alexander called from down the hall. Keera O'Quinn quickly saved her progress on her unfinished novel and closed the lid of her laptop. Her roommate had just finished her last final and they were set to walk at graduation. Grinning when Ness appeared in the open doorway of their dorm room, Keera stood.

"Well?" she asked.

"Guess what just came in the mail!" Nessa pulled out a padded envelope and shook it back in forth in excitement.

"You got it?" Keera jumped up and down. "I'm so happy!"

Nessa pulled the tab at the top and the envelope made its usual tearing sound. Then Ness peered inside. Reverently pulling out the dark blue booklet, she sighed.

"It's so pretty."

"It's a passport, sweetie, not a diamond," Keera teased.

"Easy for you to say," Ness replied. "You've travelled all

over the world. I've lived exactly two places. Indianapolis and here."

"Now, the world is your oyster, so they say."

Ness's face screwed up in a cute way. "I don't like oysters."

Both women giggled and as Ness bounded over to her bunk and sat bouncing on it, Keera opened the small waist high refrigerator, pulling out a cheap bottle of sparkling wine.

"When did you get that?" Ness gasped.

"Yesterday, while you finished your neo-classical literature final. I knew we could celebrate. So," she popped the cork, filled two paper cups, and headed over to her best friend. "How did your last final go?"

"Ugh," Ness groaned. "New Age Lit is a pain in my butt. I just can't understand it all. Classics are the ones for me."

"The term is arse, Ness, it's okay to curse about New Age lit," Keera laughed. They clanked their cups together and drank.

"So good," Ness replied closing her eyes, savoring the champagne. "What about you? How did Marketing four-oh-four go?"

"Not terrible," she replied. "The presentation portion made up most of our grade and the slides were a hit, if I do say so myself."

"Was it weird finishing the project with Max?" she asked.

"Nah, we're still friends," Keera replied. "Besides our split was a mutual decision. But he may have congratulated me privately afterwards."

"Ooh, you are way too adventurous for me," Ness shook her head and sipped her drink.

"It was amazing," Keera answered. "He is really talented with certain areas."

"TMI, babe," Ness giggled.

"Oh, come on, like you aren't curious," Keera teased. "How you remained celibate all through college is amazing to me."

"Never found someone I wanted to be with."

"We'll have to find you a hot Irishman while you're visiting with me. There are so many single guys in the main cities, it's like you could have your pick!"

"I've stocked up on my Irish romance novels," Ness admitted. "I'll live in a dreamworld until my man shows up."

"Yeah, Irishmen are gentlemen in the streets and beasts between the sheets."

"Kee!" Nessa blushed red hot and looked away, then drained her champagne. "There's not enough champagne in the world to prepare me for this conversation."

"Just trust me on this, babe," she said.

"I do," Ness answered. "Speaking of Irishmen…" Ness waited until Keera refilled her cup. "Whatever happened to you and the guy you were hot and heavy with over there? I remember you wouldn't miss a single call from him the first few months then it started to taper off and you met Dylan. I'm sorry but I don't remember his name."

"Yeah," Keera looked away. "Paddy… Paddy O'Shea, he's my cousin's best friend. He's also a secret."

"What? Why?" Ness asked.

"Because my cousin Emmet would kill him if he found out."

"Is he a bad guy?"

"No," Keera defended. "He's just known as a player. We met a few years ago at a party and when I turned eighteen, we decided to give it a go. My birthday gift from him was… him." Paddy's face flashed in her mind, his easy smile, drownable eyes, and twinkling smile. But then the all-consuming mortification of the morning after and every time he called it quits when it was getting too deep, stopped her fantasy.

"I'm sorry, honey," Ness reached out and covered her hand with hers. "Did he hurt you?"

"No," Keera hurried to explain, stopping Ness from reliving her own past with her stepfather. "He was… is amazing and will always be the man I love but…" Keera shook her head and forced the sad thoughts aside. "I fully intend on hooking up with him while I'm home."

Ness smiled slightly and Keera knew better than to force happiness with her best friend. Ness knew her better than anyone, save her mother and cousin, Emmet. Even having only met their first day on campus two years ago, Keera counted her freckly faced, redheaded, American friend as a sister.

"Listen, in two weeks, we fly to Ireland and if I can't get you a boyfriend by the time of my cousin Sean's wedding in a month, then I'm a crappy best friend."

Ness' smile bloomed. "Deal," she raised her cup and tapped it against Keera's then drank.

But no matter how hard she tried, she couldn't get Paddy's face out of her head all evening, all week, and the long month back in County Clare.

Perhaps she could sneak out and see him while everyone was at Sheehan's pub in Killarney. It would be the first time in two years. It had to be perfect.

Chapter One

Three weeks later

"Men are gobshites honey, I'm sorry," Keera stated, wrapping her friend in her arms.

"Oh, tanks very much," Emmet grumbled.

"Cheers," Paddy said from behind the counter. Keera resisted looking over at him. It was the first time she had seen him and even though they had been texting all week, she had yet to hold him, smell his musky cologne, or feel his silky hair beneath her fingertips. But her cousin Emmet was right there and if she looked over at his best friend, he would know something was up.

"Emmet told me what happened," Keera went on. "I can't believe that arsehole!"

"Kee, it's okay," Ness soothed.

"No, it's not," Keera said, her anger over the situation with her cousin Sean taking precedence. "But listen, I'll pack you some things when I get back. We'll go down to Dublin and get us a couple hot barmen. We'll flirt the night away. Oh, and we'll have Emmet to make sure no guy gets too close."

She risked a glance at Paddy then, only to see him looking down at the computer, his jaw was set and his eyes hard.

"Oh?" Emmet asked drawing her attention. "And what if I want to leave early to have me own fun?"

Keera waved him off. "We all know you've been celibate since Chloe."

Emmet stared at her and she tried not to laugh at the shock and horror on his face. "Right, 'cause *that's* normal."

Ness laughed and Keera turned back to her best friend. "Anyway, stay here for a little, go see the Ring and Emmet will look after you. Get Sean out of your head."

Ness nodded and after a quick hug, Keera headed to the door. She could feel Paddy's eyes on her. Hearing the elevator ding, she paused just inside the vestibule and looked back. Ness and Emmet were in the elevator and the doors were closing. Paddy was watching her, his light brown eyes suggestive and her body burned. Peeking back in, she moved her head indicating outside and he nodded.

It had been far too long. Too long without Keera. When he saw her breeze into the lobby of the hotel he worked in as carefree as she did everything, Paddy nearly gave the whole thing away. Wanting to jump over the counter, which would have been a feat in itself as the counter was well over four feet tall, race to her and kiss her senseless, Paddy tampered his initial reaction. Emmet, his best friend and sometimes boss at the car dealer, was standing right beside the young woman Paddy was helping get two rooms for the night. Initially, when the striking young woman came in asking for two rooms and dropping Emmet's name, Paddy wanted to tease. They both brought conquests back to the hotel, it was the best place since no one wanted to give out addresses to a potential one-night stand. But when he saw her tear-lined, red rimmed eyes, he refrained and was glad he did. Apparently, the girl had been hurt. Then in she walked; looking gorgeous and sexy as hell.

Once all the fluff was through and Keera turned away from them all, Paddy waited to call to her. He needed to make sure no one knew about them and since Emmet used to work at the Plaza Hotel, he still had friends. Seeing her wait inside the vestibule, made his palms sweaty and his blood pressure skyrocket. Her little nod to outside, made his heart jump. Cursing his reaction, he reminded himself he was a confirmed bachelor like his Uncle Tully, even if thirty-three years separated them.

But it was Keera O'Quinn.

He felt differently about her, always had and that thought scared him.

Asking his coworker to take over the front desk, he stepped out the employee's entrance, and saw Keera waiting in the shadows.

"Gobshites? Really, Kee?" he teased, and it felt good to be back to their old rhythm. The sheepish grin that spread over her lips lit her eyes and made his chest ache.

"Why not? It's true. Prove me wrong," she stepped closer to him.

In an instant, he had her pinned to the wall with his body and his lips on hers. Growling, he pushed his tongue into her mouth to duel with hers. She rubbed her hands up and down his chest, growing bolder than ever before. He pulled back with a curse.

"Damn," he said. "I've missed you, Keera."

"Why didn't you come to Blarney Castle earlier?" she asked in-between kisses.

"I had to work, love," he replied. "I've been here since noon."

"Too bad," she moved to his neck and he sucked on the tender spot just behind her ear. Her breath shuddered. "I had the perfect spot picked out."

"To do what?" he coaxed.

"To show you how much I've missed you."

He groaned and instantly there were too many layers between them. He pulled off his suit jacket and her coat.

"We don't have much time, so you're going to have to make it quick," she breathed, helping unbutton his shirt.

"We have all the time in the world."

"I have a beer and a cig waiting for me."

"Since when did you pick smoking back up?" Paddy asked.

"Since there's a right wetser of a man waiting for me."

An unfamiliar emotion bubbled to the surface and before he could suppress it, he pulled away and looked her in the eye. The ugly truth sunk in. She was only there for a quick hookup. His stomach plummeted and his heart slowed. He meant nothing to her.

"So what? I'm just another piece of fun for you?" he demanded. She looked at him then burst out laughing. Pulling away from the wall, he began buttoning up his shirt and tucking it into his pants.

"Do I need to remind you about our first time? *My* first time? You left in the morning without so much as a goodbye."

"That was then," he justified grabbing his jacket off a couple pallets used by the kitchen staff.

"And now is different?" She questioned. He looked back at her; her flushed cheeks, red lips, and mussed hair. She was so beautiful and yet the jealousy stung, giving their reunion an agonizing end. "You were very clear you weren't looking for anything and no commitment was made before I left," she reminded him.

"What do you expect from me? You come here; I haven't seen you in two years. I read your signals. I come out here and you only want me to hurry up so you can go back to another man waiting for you? What do you expect me to feel?"

"There's nothing permanent with us, Paddy," she replied. "You don't want anything more. Why would you care if I have another guy or two waiting for me?"

"Dammit, Keera, you aren't supposed to be like that."

"Like what?" she demanded.

"Like all the others. I thought you were different. Special. And here you are, just like everyone else."

"You were the one who told me you didn't want a relationship! You never said anything in all the texts, calls, hell even emails, that you wanted anything more."

"I don't."

"Then forgive me if I don't quite understand what you're trying to say. We have never had a relationship. It's a good time between two people who are attracted to each other. That's it, or do you not remember your words to me before I left for America?" She grabbed her handbag and headed down the alley.

"Keera," he called but she didn't respond, instead she kept walking. "Keera."

"What, Paddy?" she whirled around.

"I..." he couldn't say the words. They were on his tongue, but he couldn't breathe them to life.

She licked her lips and he saw the telltale shimmer in her eyes. "That's what I thought." Without another word, she turned back down the alley and out of sight.

After a moment, Paddy raced after her only to see her joining a group of men out front of Sheehan's. One of them greeted her with a smack on the arse and a beer, another offered her a cigarette. Paddy growled. But Keera laughed and took the man's cigarette with a suggestive wink. The one who gave her a beer, leaned in and his lips moved near her ear, but Paddy couldn't hear nor see what he was saying. But Keera grinned and after a puff, she took the man's hand and they walked around the side of the pub to another darkened alley.

Paddy knew exactly what was going to happen and he took two steps forward to stop it but froze. They had fun, always did. But when she told him over the phone, she wanted to see other people while in America, his image of the future with her in it, shattered. He remembered that day. His Uncle Tully pulling him back from the figurative edge. Pulling out his phone again, he dialed quickly.

"Paddy, my boy," his uncle's familiar voice rang over the phone. "How are ya?"

"She's gone, Uncle Tully. I had her in my grasp and I screwed up... again. I..."

"Tell me what happened, lad," his familiar smooth baritone grounding him. Tully was the only one he had ever told. When Paddy and Keera were together for the first time, her first time, he had held her to him as she slept and after kissing her temple, had said three words to her he never told another partner.

I love you.

And it had scared the shite out of him

Chapter
Two

Fifteen Months Later

Keera stared down at the pregnancy test as her hand shook. The double lines blurred as she swayed. How could she be pregnant? She took every precaution. She couldn't be. It had to be a false positive. There was no possible way... but there was... Her on-again-off-again boyfriend; Patrick O'Flannery and she had been more on than off in recent months, even if they had broken up for good a month ago. But her missed cycle and the two lines on the stick, clearly showed he had left something with her.

She screeched when someone knocked on the door.

"Sweetheart, are you all right?" her mother called.

"Fine, ma," she answered through the closed door, her voice only wavering slightly.

"All right, darling, well, hurry up. Your Aunt Dee just called. We need to head over. Emmet has something to share with us all."

"I'm really not feeling well, ma. Can you go and tell me what it is?"

"Oh sweetie, I'm sorry was it something you ate?"

"No," then she thought better of it. "Maybe," she fibbed. "I don't know."

"Well, you know I would honey but Emmet need our support right now. It might be about the hearing for his son. Come on, maybe some fresh air will do you good."

Keera knew she was right, but she couldn't bear going to see her family especially not the ferry ride. The mere thought of it made her want to vomit up her breakfast. But the drive alone with her mom was what she didn't want. Her mother was so perceptive, she would know something was wrong and she just couldn't bring herself to tell her mom who, twenty-three years ago, had been in that very bathroom vomiting and crying over a positive pregnancy test. She just couldn't tell her. Siobhan had sacrificed so much so Keera wouldn't end up like her but, what happened? Some stupid boy, that's what, and not the boy she wanted either.

Shaking her head, she hadn't seen Paddy since that night in Killarney where she first met Patrick O'Flannery. She didn't want to admit she missed him. She didn't want to admit she still had dreams of laying with him in Killarney Park on a beautifully warm day, having a picnic and making love under the shade of a tree.

He meant something to her, she would be the first one to admit it, but he had never come after her. He was a stubborn bastard, that much was clear, but she had hoped... no, it wasn't going to happen, but she hoped he would come back to her.

Splashing cold water on her face, she took several deep breaths and forced herself to smile. Opening the door, she saw her mom down the hall scurrying around in the kitchen.

"Ma? What are you doing?" she asked.

Her mom turned to her. "Oh, honey, you look so pale. Are you sure you're all right?"

"I'm fine," she answered quickly. "What's with the take-aways?"

"Well, I figured whatever you got into should be in last night's dinner so I'm tossing it out."

"No, ma, it's not from dinner last night."

"You don't know, honey, better safe than sorry."

Safe... she thought was being safe. Apparently not.

"Ma, it's not the food," she said.

"Was it the chips?" she asked, not listening and still moving around the kitchen.

"Ma, no."

"What about the beans from yesterday's breakfast? It could have been them. They smell off to me."

"I'm pregnant," Keera finally said.

There was a crash behind the open refrigerator door, then silence. Finally, Siobhan walked out into Keera's view. Her face was pale and blank.

"What did you say, love?" she finally asked.

"I'm pregnant, ma. I'm so sorry." Keera finally burst into tears.

Siobhan raced to her daughter and grabbed her tightly in her arms. Keera cried harder into her mother's chest. Throughout her tears, her mother held her close, speaking softly but letting her cry. When Keera finally calmed enough, she pulled slightly away but Siobhan led her over to the couch.

Sitting together after Siobhan grabbed some tissues, Keera dried her eyes and picked at the remaining tissues. Her mother softly stroked her back, giving her a chance to calm down.

"I'm sorry, ma," she finally said. "I took every precaution but somehow..."

"Nothing is one hundred percent, sweetie," her mom replied. "Which test did you do?"

"I got one from a place in Ennis. I didn't want anyone to know. I just took it."

"How late are you?"

"I missed last month but I didn't think anything of it then. I was supposed to start a week ago, that's when I realized I hadn't..."

"Is it Paddy's?" she asked gently.

Keera's eyes shot up to her mom. She and Paddy had agreed not to tell anyone for fear of her cousins' reactions.

"Sweetie, I wasn't born yesterday, I've been there. I've also seen the looks between you both. I'm guessing you've been together since before you went to America.

"We... we were but... it's been a while and I'm with Patrick O'Flannery now... on and off."

"Does he know?" she asked. Keera shook her head.

"We broke up... for good this time, last month."

"And there's no one else?"

Keera shook her head again. "I'm so sorry, ma. I know how much you've sacrificed for me trying to get me to school and a good job. I'm so sorry."

"Sweetie, my one concern is *you*. Yes, it's not ideal but, honey, I love you. Now, we need to set a time to meet with a doctor. You got this and I will be with you every step of the way."

"I don't know, ma. I don't think I can do this. I'm not like you. I'm not as strong as you were."

"You are, and I wasn't very strong, sweetie. Your gran and grandad helped me so much. I'll never forget how they took care of me. You'll always have me, sweetie. And I'm going to tell you what my mother told me, all right? She said *rejoice, that's a new life you're bringing into the world. Not everyone gets to feel their baby grow inside them, some women will never feel the sheer love of being able to hold your newborn in your arms.* Some women try and try only for disappointment. You were chosen to bring this life into the world. You get to enjoy those moments. Celebrate it. It's nothing to be ashamed of, it's something to be so grateful for."

"You'll help me?" she begged.

"Whenever and however you need me, love, always," Siobhan smiled and tucked a strand of hair behind her ear. "I do think you need to tell Patrick. He deserves to know. He is the father."

Keera violently shook her head. "No, I can't. He won't want the baby. I know he won't."

"You don't know that until you ask."

"I can't marry him."

"No one said anything about marriage, love. But he has a right to know."

"Did you... did you tell the man who fathered me?" Keera asked.

"Yes, I did," she replied. "But my experience isn't the same as yours could be."

"He didn't want me, did he?"

"That's not true, love," she sighed. "You've never asked about your da' before."

"I've not been pregnant before..."

"Touché," she answered. "He was not in a position where he could do anything about it. And if I told anyone else, his life would be ruined. I loved him. I couldn't tell."

"He was married, wasn't he?" Keera asked.

Siobhan took a deep breath and nodded. "My professor. But he wasn't terrible, honey. He was concerned and he was there for me when he could be."

"But he didn't attempt to be in my life at all."

"He couldn't," Siobhan shook her head.

"Why not? Didn't he want to meet me? At all?"

"Yes, of course he did," Siobhan replied. "But... he couldn't. I wouldn't let him. He had so much to lose."

"And what about me? I've lived my entire life without my father."

"I know," she looked down.

"Do you still talk to him?" Keera asked.

"No," Siobhan revealed. "I haven't since you turned eighteen and I asked him to come to your party. He couldn't or wouldn't. And that was it. But enough about that. I know it's not ideal, but Deirdre was very anxious that we get there before noon." She kissed her daughter's forehead and cupped her face. "Go and get dressed. We'll swing by my doctor's office on the way back. He is very nice, and I'll talk to them. See about getting you in today. Let him do a test again and get you on some prenatal vitamins."

Keera huffed a sigh and agreed, hurrying down the hallway to her room.

Paddy stared at Emmet for a long minute.

"Are you taking a piss? First, you tell me you're marrying this lash then you tell me I'm going to have to work with *Tom Callahan*? You swore to castrate anyone who spoke his name and now you're wanting him to work here?"

"He needs a job," Emmet explained. "And I never said I'd

castrate anyone. I was langered if I did. But aye, he's going to work here. Today is his first day and I need you to train him."

"Train him? Go way outta that."

"Paddy, I need you. You're me best salesman. Please."

"Ah, hell, flattery will get you everywhere, O'Quinn. Fine. But you owe me a pint."

"Make it two," Emmet agreed and slapped him on the shoulder. "Cheers, mate."

"Lay off," Paddy replied. "What time is he going to be here?"

"I told him ten, so any minute," Emmet stated.

"Boss," another salesman knocked on Emmet's open door. "Tom Callahan is here. Says he has a meeting with you?" the man's eyes were wide, and Paddy didn't miss how he shielded his lower region with his hand when he said the name.

"Aye, cheers, thank you. Have him come in," Emmet replied then turned to Paddy. "Thank you, Paddy. I owe you one."

Nodding once, they both looked to the door when Tom knocked.

"Tom! Good to see ya," Emmet pulled him into an embrace and Paddy thought for sure the cameras would descend. He had to be on some crazy show. There was no way Emmet O'Quinn and Tom Callahan were talking again, let alone embracing.

"Thanks for having me," Tom replied and looked over at Paddy.

"You remember Paddy O'Shea, two years behind us in Primary?" Emmet reintroduced.

"Yeah of course," Tom answered and stuck out a hand for him to shake. Paddy shook himself out of his stupor and took the hand.

"Good to see you again, Tom," Paddy said. "Welcome."

"Cheers, thanks," Tom replied.

"Paddy will be your trainer; any questions just ask."

"Great, thanks for agreeing to helping me."

"No worries, you'll learn quickly. Ehm, let's start with the breakroom." Paddy offered to have Tom go ahead of him and then glanced back at Emmet. His friend had a smile on his face that hadn't left his lips since he first met Mara McGrath. Paddy rolled his eyes and joined Tom in the hall.

Chapter Three

One Week Later

Keera's hand shook as she and Siobhan waited in the hospital. Seeing Emmet shot on the steps of the courthouse would stay with her for the rest of her life. Then, for Ness to go into labor... she shook her head to clear it. Her mom brought her some herbal tea and smiled slightly.

"They'll both be fine, love," she said as she sat beside her. "Ness is young and strong. She'll have that precious baby in her arms in no time. Don't you worry."

"I'm not," she said, though to be honest, she was. In a few short months she could be experiencing the same thing. Monday she and her mom had stopped in at the local doctor who took a urine sample but didn't have the lab needed and had to send it out. It would take two to three days for the results and that's if they moved quickly; which knowing country doctors wouldn't happen. Keera almost wished they had gone to Dublin to have the test done there. The old doctor assured her, store bought pregnancy tests weren't always accurate. But she knew in her heart she was. Blowing on the hot tea, she sipped it and hummed.

"Thanks, ma," she said.

"You're welcome, sweetie. Any news on Emmet?"

"Nothing yet," she breathed. "To see him like that. I—"

"I know," her mom said but the sound of her voice cracking made Keera look over at her.

"He'll be okay, ma," she said.

Siobhan nodded and patted her cheek. Ever since before Keera was born, her mom was close to all her nephews. When their mother died, Siobhan took on the mantle but that was after Keera was born and not easy for her.

Orin and Deirdre, Emmet's father and stepmother, walked down the hall to them and Siobhan and Keera stood.

"Anything?" Siobhan asked.

"He's still in surgery," Orin stated but Keera saw the tightness around her uncle's eyes and mouth.

Deirdre patted her eyes dry. "We just came from Sean's and Ness's room. Her contractions are about five minutes apart and she's dilated about five centimeters. They're going to be a while."

"How's Sean holding up?" Innis asked walking up to them, a cup of cappuccino in his hand.

"He's not doing great," Deirdre revealed. "He's worried but not showing it to Ness. And he's worried about his brother."

"I'll go talk to him," Innis offered, and Orin took him

down the hall toward the maternity ward.

Deirdre sat with them and allowed Siobhan to take her hand. Leaning her head back against the wall, she sighed.

"Please tell me some good news, something to get my mind off my boy fighting for his life," Deirdre begged.

Siobhan looked over at Keera but said nothing. "How's Sinéad?" Siobhan asked after Deirdre's daughter.

"She's scared, but she went home with Rachel and Trish. She was worn out from crying, poor lamb."

"It's been five hours, surely they know something by now," Keera demanded and stood.

"Cabhan said it could take a long time, honey," Deirdre said.

"But they should tell us something," she began to pace.

"Keera," her mom cautioned. "Calm down, honey. Stress is not good for the—" she stopped herself when Keera turned wide eyes on her mom.

"Baby?" Deirdre intuitively finished. She jumped up and rushed to Keera. "Sweetie, are you pregnant?"

"I—"

"Oh honey, I'm so happy!" Deirdre pulled her into a bone-breaking hug. "When are you due?"

"I—"

Someone cleared their throat behind them, and Deirdre pulled away and looked at who had arrived. When Keera locked eyes with Paddy O'Shea, her stomach dropped. Paddy looked damn good, dressed to the nines. He wore a suit, different from his uniform at the Plaza Hotel. His dark auburn almost brown hair was brushed and soft, his jaw was covered in a week's worth of stubble but his light brown eyes stared holes through her.

He said nothing but Keera knew he had heard her aunt.

"Paddy," her mother said with a smile, standing and heading over to him. "It's good to see you again."

"And you, Ms. O'Quinn," he said finally pulling his eyes from Keera to greet her. "I heard about Emmet. I wanted to check on him."

"He's still in surgery, Paddy. Thank you, love," Deirdre explained.

"Do they have any idea what happened?" Paddy asked, not looking at her.

"He was shot twice in the chest by Mara's ex-boyfriend. He fell onto the steps holding Trevor, his son. The little one is all right, but Emmet lost a lot of blood and they're worried about the location of the bullets. One is at his sternum and the other is... directly below his heart. They said it's a miracle it didn't go right through it. He's in surgery but the outlook is... grim," Deirdre explained, tears again gathering in the corners of her eyes.

"Did they catch this guy?" Paddy asked.

"Yes," Deirdre answered. "He's in custody but no one has seen Mara since it happened."

Keera's ears were ringing and as much as she tried to focus on the rest of the conversation, she stared at Paddy. Watching him, waiting for him to look at her, and when it didn't happen, she willed it but still it didn't happen.

Just once, she would have loved for him to look at her the way he had before. Just once. It would help her get through the next few years, if he only looked at her.

While she was in America, his weekly calls had been a lifeline in a new place and when they were able to Skype, it was even better but after her first year, she started taking less and less of his calls. She had her own friends and she and Ness were hanging out more and more. When she did answer, their conversation fell into an easy rhythm, but she wanted more. She wanted exciting. She wanted fun, like Paddy used to be.

When she returned from America, they continued their secret and she loved it, but as soon as he expected her to have saved herself for him when he hadn't done the same, she was done. She was tired of chauvinistic society. The man could do whatever he wanted with no consequences, but a woman slept with two or three men, she was a slut.

She and Paddy hadn't talked since that night fifteen months ago and looking at him, she realized how sorry she was for that. Patrick O'Flannery was dangerous, fun, and interesting. But he was not her ever after. Looking at Paddy O'Shea, in all his *GQ* model glory, she knew she wanted him and maybe it wasn't too late. But then she felt a fluttering in her stomach, butterflies she thought, or maybe... Paddy would never want to raise another man's child.

Is it possible for your heart to stop beating for a solid ten seconds? Paddy wondered. *If not, thank god I'm in a hospital.*

When he had heard Keera's voice, he instinctually followed the sound but as he stood there, forcing himself to listen to Deirdre tell him what happened to his dearest friend, he could not stop his thoughts.

Keera was pregnant.

For a split second he hoped it was his, but then realization overcame, and he knew it couldn't be. Then anger had surfaced, and he suppressed it. If he gave in and looked at her, he wouldn't have a chance and he would be back to the sniveling, whipped puppy she seemed to enjoy. But god help him, he wanted to look at her, he wanted to see she wasn't all right with this, with the baby, with the way things were left between them.

But he would never feel that way again. He wouldn't allow any woman to make him feel less than he was.

"The doctors are trying to be hopeful but it's the one that

nicked his lung they worry about. But at least it wasn't his heart," Deirdre finished.

Paddy nodded once. "Well, I'm glad he's going to be all right. We've closed up the dealership for the day, but I wanted to check on him."

"I'm sure he'll be glad you did," Siobhan said.

Paddy thanked her and then looked down. "I should go."

"No need, love," Deirdre replied. "It's good to see you, Paddy. Stay."

"Thank you, Mrs. O'Quinn, but I can't," he answered. He felt Keera's eyes on him the whole time and if he didn't get out of there quickly, he wasn't sure he had the will to leave again. He had prided himself on moving on with his life, putting Keera behind him, even if he wasn't fooling anyone. He hadn't been with anyone in the fifteen months they had been apart.

One glance... She looked so scared, all he wanted to do was pull her into him and keep her safe, fight all her battles.

Dear god in heaven, I still love her.

www.ingramcontent.com/pod-product-compliance
Lightning Source LLC
Chambersburg PA
CBHW052028020726
47501CB00004B/1309

* 9 7 8 0 9 9 9 8 7 0 8 1 5 *